Joni considered the cocky sideways grin Grant frequently flashed her way. The man smiled exactly as if he knew what she was thinking and his arrogant self *liked* that she wanted to rip off his clothes and lick him from head to toe and all in between.

Definitely all in between.

He expected no less than that reaction from women.

Why would he?

The man was a god when it came to the opposite sex. Women of all ages fell over themselves vying for his attention—vying for one of those half-cocked grins to be just for them.

No, he wasn't a god—more like a tempting devil, crooking his finger to lure women to the dark side.

Dear Reader

Life sometimes forces us in new directions whether we want to go there or not. When nurse Joni Thompson's heart and career are left in tatters by the man she loves, she starts over in Bean's Creek, North Carolina, making a new life for herself, determined never to give another man control over her life.

Only she can't resist Dr Grant Bradley's smile—nor his touch. But so long as she's the one making the rules and they stick to them her heart and job will be safe...right? Too bad the dashing pulmonologist is playing by his own set of life rules—rules that leave her heart vulnerable. But what's a girl to do when he steals her breath and demands she give him her all?

Hope you enjoy Joni and Grant's story, and the Bean's Creek crew.

I love to hear from readers. Please e-mail me at janice@janicelynn.net to let me know what you think of Joni and Grant's story, or just to chat about romance. You can also visit me at www.janicelynn.net, or on Facebook, to find out my latest news.

Happy reading!

Janice

CHALLENGING THE NURSE'S RULES

BY
JANICE LYNN

MILLS & BOON

First published in Great Britain 2012
by Mills & Boon, an imprint of Harlequin (UK) Limited.
Large Print edition 2013
Harlequin (UK) Limited, Eton House,
18-24 Paradise Road, Richmond, Surrey TW9 1SR

© Janice Lynn 2012

ISBN: 978 0 263 23094 9

Harlequin (UK) policy is to use papers that are
natural, renewable and recyclable products and made
from wood grown in sustainable forests. The logging
and manufacturing process conform to the legal
environmental regulations of the country of origin.

Printed and bound in Great Britain
by CPI Antony Rowe, Chippenham, Wiltshire

Janice Lynn has a Masters in Nursing from Vanderbilt University, and works as a nurse practitioner in a family practice. She lives in the southern United States with her husband, their four children, their Jack Russell—appropriately named Trouble—and a lot of unnamed dust bunnies that have moved in since she started her writing career.

To find out more about Janice and her writing visit www.janicelynn.com

Recent titles by the same author:

FLIRTING WITH THE SOCIETY DOCTOR
DOCTOR'S DAMSEL IN DISTRESS
THE NURSE WHO SAVED CHRISTMAS
OFFICER, GENTLEMAN…SURGEON!
DR DI ANGELO'S BABY BOMBSHELL
PLAYBOY SURGEON, TOP-NOTCH DAD

These books are also available in eBook format from www.millsandboon.co.uk

To the crew at Dr. J Family Medicine.
Thank you for making me a part of your family.
I love you all.

CHAPTER ONE

"THERE is just something about that man that makes my uterus want to come out of retirement."

Intensive Care nurse Joni Thompson's gaze jerked away from the IV pump she was programming to gawk at the eighty-plus-year-old skeleton of a woman lying in the hospital bed. Mrs. Sain had severe chronic obstructive pulmonary disease and was unfortunately a frequent flyer in the ICU when she lapsed into hypercapneic respiratory failure.

Joni didn't have to ask who her patient referred to. Apparently, even little old ladies two tiptoed steps from death's doorway weren't immune to his charm.

Dr. Grant Bradley, pulmonologist extraordinare. Okay, so the man had it all. Brains, beauty, body. Not that she'd noticed.

Much.

Oh, yes, much perfectly described how she'd not noticed Grant.

She'd not noticed much about his sky-blue eyes. Or much about his broad shoulders that couldn't be hidden beneath his standard hospital-issue scrub tops that perfectly matched those thickly lashed intelligent eyes. Or much about his narrow hips, and she just knew if she could pull his scrub pants tight to his body, he'd have a butt not worth much ado as well.

But his smile was what she'd not noticed the most much.

His smile lit up his face, dug dimples into his handsome cheeks, and made his beautiful eyes dance with mischief. The man's smile did funny things to her insides.

She closed her eyes and willed Grant out of her head yet again. Seemed like the longer he worked in Bean's Creek, the more she had to forcibly exorcise the man from her thoughts.

"It's his smile, you know."

Had Mrs. Sain read her mind or what?

Joni gawked at the white-haired woman fanning her face as if she really was having a full-blown hot flush brought on by a sudden surge of Dr. Grant Bradley-is-Hot hormones.

"When that man smiles it's as if he knows your every secret." Mrs. Sain's fanning increased, gaining good rhythm for a person in her frail condition. "As if he knows you're thinking about him, and he likes being the center of your attention." A soft sigh escaped thin, pale lips as her eyes closed. "Reminds me of my Hickerson."

Joni smiled at the woman's reminiscing of her late husband. Her patient often mentioned the devilishly handsome man she'd spent more than sixty-five years married to.

Was Mrs. Sain right? Was it Grant's smile that made him so irresistible? Joni considered the cocky sideways grin he frequently flashed her way. The man smiled exactly as if he knew what she was thinking and his arrogant self liked it that she wanted to rip off his clothes and lick him from head to toe and all in between.

Definitely all in between.

He expected no less than that reaction from women.

Why would he?

The man was a god when it came to the opposite sex. Women of all ages fell over themselves vying for his attention, vying for one of those half-cocked grins to be just for them.

No, he wasn't a god, more like a tempting devil crooking his finger to lure women to the dark side.

Biting back a frustrated sigh, Joni shook her head at her still fanning—although rapidly losing momentum—patient. The woman had been on a vent less than forty-eight hours before. If Joni didn't know better she'd swear the IV fluid must have contained youth serum. Or one hundred-proof estrogen. Joni really liked the spunky older lady who somehow always managed to bounce back no matter how ill she was at time of admission.

"Not that he looks at me like that, mind you. But I've seen how he looks at you." Mrs. Sain placed her weathered hand on Joni's arm. "I think he may be a little sweet on you."

"I think your oxygen must be dropping because you obviously aren't thinking straight,"

Joni snorted, winking to soften her words because she'd been a bit more brusque than she'd meant to. Honestly, she just couldn't deal with Grant being "a little sweet" on her. She had her once messy life all straightened out. She didn't need Dr. Steal Her Breath throwing a curve into her life plan.

Mrs. Sain didn't appear in the slightest concerned about her oxygen levels, just laughed at Joni's remark and patted her arm with thin, clubbed fingers.

Trying her best not to react so she didn't encourage Mrs. Sain's current train of thought, Joni listened to the woman's heart and lungs. She noted the steady click of the woman's pacemaker and the coarse rhonchi and expiratory wheezing heard bibasilarly in both lungs anteriorly and posteriorly. As horrible as the woman's lungs sounded, they were still much improved from even the day before. Hopefully her breathing would continue to improve so Grant could discharge her back to the assisted living facility where she resided.

Grant sweet on her? Only in Joni's secret late-night fantasies was a man like Grant sweet on her.

No, that wasn't true. For some unknown reason Grant was interested in her. Although he'd seemed a bit standoffish with her at first, for the past few weeks he'd found reasons to seek her out, talk to her, touch her arm or hand, to make eye contact and smile that wicked smile at her.

He had asked her out.

For this weekend.

She'd immediately turned him down. Not that he'd accepted that. No, the great Dr. Bradley had told her to think about it because they both knew she wanted to go out with him as much as he wanted her to say yes.

Ha! Who was he to say that she wanted to go out with him?

How much did he want her to say yes? Why?

If she had said yes, go where?

He hadn't even told where their supposed date would have been. Most likely the hospital's Hearts for Health fundraiser.

The last thing she wanted was to go to a hospital event and be lumped into the category of Dr. Bradley's latest bedroom babe.

No matter how long she thought about his question, no matter how tempted she might be, her answer wouldn't change.

She knew all about men like Grant. They played the field then moved on, leaving havoc in their wake. Grant was no different. Hadn't he already made his way through a good portion of the single population at the hospital?

Okay, so technically she only knew of a couple of hospital employees he'd been linked with during the few months he'd been in Bean's Creek, but there were probably more, right? It wasn't as if she was privy to his social calendar, but she imagined the man never lacked for female company.

She imagined lots of things in regard to Grant.

So okay, he was interested and, truth be told, she thought about him a lot. Too much really. But she wouldn't be changing her mind about going out with him. She knew better. Had learned that lesson the hard way years ago.

Dr. Mark Braseel had taught her well.

"I think you might be a little sweet on him, too."

Mrs. Sain's words had the effect of hot lava dropping onto Joni's face. Was her annoying fascination with the man that obvious? How long had she been in a thinking-of-Grant daze? No wonder he'd asked her out. He probably thought she was an easy score to add another notch to his proverbial macho-man belt.

No, thank you. Been there, done that. Not ever walking down that painful road again regardless of how much Grant might tempt her. Some scars ran too deep to risk reopening.

She met Mrs. Sain's curious gaze, held it without blinking. "You couldn't be further from the truth."

Which was true. None of her thoughts about Grant were sweet. If she were on that hot-blooded man, well, let's just say she wouldn't be sweet. Uh-uh, no way. She'd be a wildcat.

Hello! Where had that come from? Her? A wildcat?

She laughed out loud at the mere thought of her being wild, period. Not her. She was the perpetual good girl. The one and only time she'd stepped outside her good-girl shoes she'd paid too high a price.

A stab of pain pierced her chest and she blinked away the moisture that stung her eyes at the memory of her life's biggest mistake. She'd been so gullible, so stupid. No way would she ever let a man deceive her like that again.

"Now, Mrs. Sain, let's get back to important things. Like your health." She bit the inside of her lower lip, tasting the metallic tang of blood. Telling herself to get a grip, she refocused on the IV pump settings. "I'm so glad that your lungs are holding their own. Although they are still weak, you're doing wonderful to be so soon off the ventilator. Your saturations are staying in the low nineties."

"Only because of this." Mrs. Sain gestured to the nasal cannula that provided a continuous flow of concentrated oxygen. "But I'm not going to complain because at least I'm breathing without that tube down my throat."

"What are you not complaining about?" the

subject of their earlier conversation asked as he invaded the room.

Invaded was the right word.

When Grant stepped into a room he encompassed and overwhelmed everyone and everything, all without putting forth any more effort than just existing. The man exuded charisma. Life could be so unfair.

"My oxygen." Mrs. Sain beamed at her doctor, encompassed and overwhelmed and obviously once again considering bringing her female organs out of retirement.

Grateful that her patient hadn't elaborated on what they'd been discussing, Joni tried to keep from looking directly at Grant. Keeping her gaze off his gorgeous face proved impossible. In mere seconds she was watching him grin at Mrs. Sain before he placed his stethoscope to her, carefully auscultating the crackling sounds the shallow rise and fall of her frail chest made.

Whatever his flaws might be—and she was sure he had a few even if she'd yet to really discover what they might be other than that he was a playboy—the man was an excellent doctor, one Joni would like on her side if her lungs ever failed.

Hello! Her lungs were failing right now, clearly not bringing in enough oxygen because when he looked up and their gazes met, she'd swear she felt…something. Something hot and intense and so powerful that she had to look away. Had to.

Because she felt encompassed and overwhelmed and as if her own uterus was doing cartwheels, wanting to come out of the self-imposed retirement Joni had forced her body into after Mark.

Because she felt as if she needed that ventilator her patient had not so long ago been weaned off.

She closed her eyes, sucked a deep breath into her starved lungs, touched the raised bed railing to ground herself to reality.

"Joni," Grant acknowledged her presence. Or maybe he wanted her to look back up at him. Or maybe he thought she was about to pass out. She didn't know. She didn't look or faint. Thank goodness.

Okay, so there was a little something-something between them. A little something-something that was hot and intense and quite potent.

She had felt it the first time she'd laid eyes on him. Yes, she had caught him looking at her several times as well, but she'd decided he must be trying to figure out why she was always looking at him.

When he was distracted, she did look.

Look? More like let her eyes feast on him, soaking up every morsel of his eye-candiness. Which meant she was quite pathetic and not nearly as immune to his charms as she liked to think. Then again, maybe she was just trying to figure out what it was about the man that messed with her head when she'd been getting along just fine all these years without once being tempted to get involved in another relationship.

"You sure got quiet." Mrs. Sain practically cackled with her delight. Definitely, her eyes held a knowing sparkle and an *uh-hum, I knew* it gleam.

Suppressing a smile in spite of her inner turmoil, Joni shook her head at the older woman who'd come so far in such a short time. "You sure talk a lot for someone who was just taken off a vent a couple of days ago. Shouldn't you be quiet? Save your voice?" she teased.

Her eyes not losing their twinkle, the older woman attempted to take a deep breath into her diseased lungs. She only managed to bring on a coughing spell that lasted a full minute and had both Grant and Joni leaning her forward to beat on her back before she calmed and nodded. "You should spend some time with me when I'm not hacking up a lung."

Glad the coughing spell had ended, Joni thought she'd like spending time with this feisty woman very much. "I'd love to."

Grant said something from behind Joni. She couldn't make out his words, but then he spoke clearer, louder to his patient. "You keep improving the way you have over the past forty-eight hours and you're going to blow this joint in a few days."

Mrs. Sain's scarce eyelashes batted coyly at Grant. "You make house calls, Doc?"

Joni suppressed an eye roll. Grant just grinned at the feisty woman.

"Only when I have a nurse to chaperone me.

Gotta have someone around to make sure I behave." He winked conspiratorially at his patient. "Maybe we can convince Joni to accompany me to check on you."

Mrs. Sain seemed to think that a brilliant idea. Joni just gave a noncommittal answer, finished logging in the data she'd collected, then skedaddled out of the hospital room before the two had her committing to something she'd regret—like making house calls with Grant.

She paused outside the closed door, took a deep breath. Phew. What was it about the man that got her so flustered?

Why ask a question she knew the answer to?

Everything about Dr. Grant Bradley flustered her—and apparently every other female on the planet.

"You are going to the Hearts for Health benefit on Friday, right?" Samantha Swann asked as she clocked out via the hospital time-keeping system on the nurses' station desktop computer.

"You know I am." Joni replaced her best friend at the computer, typed in her information, clocked out, then logged off the program. "I'm volunteer-ing with the cake walk for an hour."

The North Carolina hospital was committed to being involved within the community, play-ing an active role in helping out when needed. Hearts for Health was co-sponsored by the hos-pital, hospital employees, and local businesses to provide assistance to families with health-care needs within the community, whether that need was for transportation back and forth to doctors' appointments or for assistance with excessive medical expenses. Joni wholeheartedly believed in the organization and often volunteered a help-ing hand. Friday night was a fundraising event that involved a barbecue dinner, games, and a raf-fle for various items donated by local businesses.

"I'm selling tickets at the front door. Vann is stopping by about the time my shift ends. We'll look for you so we can all grab a bite to eat to-gether."

Vann had been Samantha's significant other since they had been fifteen. He'd asked Samantha to marry him at least a dozen times, but Saman-tha had turned him down each and every time, stating that they really shouldn't ruin a perfectly good relationship that way. As Joni couldn't name a single happily married couple, she tended to agree with her friend.

"Sounds great." She gathered her purse and turned to go, colliding into Grant.

He reached out, steadied her, smiled down at her even as she pulled away from him. How long had he been standing behind her? Had he been listening to she and Samantha talk? Why was her heart clamoring its way out of her chest? Not because his body had felt strong and solid against her. Not because in that brief moment before she'd jerked back, a zillion electrodes had sparked to life within her. Not because he'd smelled so good she'd wanted to fill her lungs with the musky scent of him.

Samantha smiled at Grant. All the nursing staff liked him. Most couldn't say enough ooey-gooey things about him.

"Is there something I can help you with before I go?" Samantha offered, despite the fact she had clocked out, doing a fairly good imitation of Mrs. Sain's earlier eyelash batting.

"No. Thanks, though." His gaze briefly touched on Samantha, then shot right back to Joni. "Can I speak with you?"

Her heart rate zoomed from banging against her ribcage to an all-out pinball machine ball ricocheting hard throughout her chest cavity. She was pretty sure her rhythm would send a cardiologist into panic, too. No way was the fluttery thump-thump in her chest anywhere near normal. Maybe she should make an appointment with Vann.

"I guess so," she squeaked, sending a desperate don't-leave-me glance toward Samantha, who proceeded to bat her lashes again, wave, and do just that. Great. Some best friend.

With a friendly nod he said goodbye to Samantha, then turned the full force of his attention onto Joni. Never had eyes been bluer or more intense. Never had a grin been more lethal. "If you're ready to go, I'll walk you to your car."

Grabbing her bag, she nodded, keeping her gaze anywhere but on him. She didn't point out that his car would be in the physicians' parking area and nowhere near hers. Neither did she point out that she was perfectly capable of walking herself to her car and that she'd been doing so for the five years she'd worked at Bean's Creek Memorial.

"What do you want to talk about?"

"Why did you say no when I asked you out?"

They asked at the same time.

Although her feet kept moving at a normal pace, the urge to run shimmied up her spine. Every fight-or-flight protective response flared strong within her body. "That's what you wanted to talk about?"

"Not really."

Surprised by his answer, her gaze cut to him. "Pardon?"

"No, I don't really want to talk about a beautiful woman saying no when I ask her to go out with me. I'd really like to forget that ever happened." He grinned sheepishly.

Joni tried to ignore the way her own eyelashes threatened to flutter at him calling her beautiful, at the impact of that smile.

"But," he continued, "I do want to understand why you said no."

Did he have all night? Because explaining her reasons could take that long if she told him the truth. If she told him about Mark, about her mother, about her fear of addiction, about how she was determined to keep her eyes focused on her career.

"Does my reason matter?" she asked instead.

"Obviously, or we wouldn't be having this conversation."

Good point. "You aren't my type."

"Male?" His eyebrows waggled in a Groucho Marx imitation.

She rolled her eyes heavenwards and kept walking.

"Good looking?"

She bit the already sore spot on her lip. The man was really too much.

"Smart?"

This time she snorted, fighting to keep from smiling. She did not want to smile. Lord knew, he didn't need any encouragement.

"Really hot in bed?"

Stopping in mid-step, Joni turned to gawk. "Seriously?"

"Seriously." The way he said the word left her in no doubt that he really was. No doubt her Egyptian cotton sheets would blaze if his naked skin ever brushed against them.

"Let me show you."

There went the smile. The one Mrs. Sain had so accurately described. The one that was making her want to say, Okay, show me, O Lucifer.

"That's not what I meant," she said instead, shaking her head, mostly because she wanted to shake loose her crazy thoughts. She was not the kind of woman who had sex with a man just because he was self-professedly "really hot in bed". "I was referring to your question in the sense of did you really just say that? Not as in 'Are you really hot in bed?'."

"Yes to both." His grin kicked up another notch, digging dimples deep into his cheeks and making laugh lines appear at the corner of his eyes. Oh, yeah, the man was Satan personified, tempting beyond belief.

"And so humble, too." She was stronger than this, better than this. Turning away from his potent smile, she began walking toward the elevator again, knowing her peace of mind lay with getting far away from him as quickly as possible. "My answer is no to both."

"Why?" he asked, easily matching her step for step.

Because you are too much like the man who broke my heart.

Because if I let you close you will break my heart, too, and I'm not ever going through that again.

Now, where had that come from? She didn't usually wear Mark as a protective shield. She usually didn't have to. No man tempted her to veer from the path she'd chosen for herself. She had responsibilities, to herself and to her mother.

"You have to ask that after what you just said to me?" she replied flippantly, not liking it that her thoughts had turned to her past. "I'm not interested, Dr. Bradley. Go be God's gift to women with someone else."

His smile slipped a little, and he sighed. "Am I coming on too strong? Is that the problem?"

Taking a deep breath, she tried a different tactic. "We both work at the hospital. You shouldn't be coming on at all."

"There aren't any hospital rules against employees dating. I checked."

Why didn't that surprise her? "I'm sure you did, several dates ago," she bit out with a little more snarkiness than she'd intended.

His brow arched. "Oh, really?"

Heat flooding her face, Joni shrugged. "I just meant that I know you've gone out with a few hospital employees."

"You know that?" He looked intrigued by her response, which she found very irritating. Everything about the man irritated her.

"I know."

His lips twisted with amusement, annoying her further. "Who is it I'm supposed to have gone out with?"

Hot faced, Joni named the women who had been linked with him. She wanted nothing more than to race the rest of the way to the elevator and escape him.

They took several steps in silence before he

said, "You know I sponsored a team in the golf tournament, right?"

No, she hadn't known that. "What golf tournament?"

"The one the Lions' club is putting on next month."

She vaguely recalled hearing something about the event, just hadn't paid much attention as she knew next to nothing about golf. "Oh." Then she frowned. "What does a golf tournament have to do with our conversation?"

"It's a co-ed tournament." His smile was lethal. "Do you know who my teammates are?" He punched the elevator down button.

She shook her head, waited for the elevator doors to slide open, and stepped inside the car, wishing by some miracle he wouldn't follow her.

Along with the hospital's medical director, he named the two women who she'd been told he was dating. The two women she'd just named.

Was he saying he hadn't dated either? Or that he'd just dated them due to the contact they shared with being teammates for the golf tournament?

"You are the only woman I've asked out on a date since I've moved to Bean's Creek."

Her heart spit and sputtered in her chest.

"You don't need to tell me any of this," she began, not quite sure why they were having this conversation or why his response made her want to throw her arms around his neck and kiss him. "For that matter, why are you telling me? What you do outside the hospital is of no consequence to me."

"See," he mused, pressing the door closed button and holding it in. His gaze held hers, refused to let her do anything more than stare back into the twinkling blue. "That's the problem. I want what I do outside the hospital to be of consequence to you."

CHAPTER TWO

SINCE when had Grant become so desperate that he had to corner a woman in an elevator to try to convince her to go on a date with him? Since when had he had to try to convince a woman to go out with him, period?

Since Joni had said no to him and he'd realized the curvy, auburn-haired beauty wasn't going to change her mind.

He'd wanted to ask her out the moment he'd arrived in Bean's Creek and met the always-smiling ICU nurse. Unfortunately, he'd learned a hard lesson about jumping into a relationship too fast. He'd wanted to be sure before he asked anyone out in Bean's Creek. To make sure he wasn't dealing with anyone mentally unstable or with addiction problems. He couldn't deal with another Ashley in his life. He'd had too much unfinished baggage to settle prior to starting a new relationship.

So he'd put his personal life on hold while he established his new practice, resolved the relationship issues he'd left behind the best he could under the circumstances, and now that he was ready to move forward, to embrace his new life, Joni had said no.

Which left him wondering why.

He'd have to be blind, deaf, and dumb not to know that she was interested in him. As interested in him as he was in her. A volatile chemistry sparked between them that threatened combustion on contact. He wasn't wrong about that. Which left what reason for her to say no?

Not that he was all that, but women didn't usually turn him down flat. Especially women who looked at him the way Joni looked at him. Had any woman ever looked at him that way? With such yearning in her eyes? He didn't think so. Which still didn't resolve the question of why she'd turned him down.

"Have I done something to offend you?" He couldn't think of anything specific, but maybe he'd inadvertently stepped on a toe or something. Maybe he should offer to rub her feet to make amends. He'd use any excuse to touch her.

She arched a brow, but didn't quite meet his eyes, more like stared at his ear or maybe a stray strand of hair. "Other than tell me you were hot in bed?"

"That offended you?" She wasn't a prude. He'd heard her laughing and cutting up with the other nurses and patients. Joni had a great sense of humor, even if she rarely gave him a direct glimpse of it. As a matter of fact, he was the only person she didn't smile at.

"Obviously, it didn't bowl me over," she pointed out, taking a step back and pressing firmly against the elevator handrail.

"Obviously." Grant regarded her long and hard and made a quick decision. "So tell me what would."

Her startled gaze shot to meet his head on. "What would what?"

"Bowl you over."

Her gaze lowered, her long lashes shading the

lovely dark green hue of her eyes. "I don't want to be bowled over."

"Perhaps not, but humor me. What would it take for a man to win your interest? No, not a man, for me to win your interest and for you to go on a date with me?"

Her cheeks flushed a bright shade of pink, splotching her creamy skin that was otherwise only marked by the spattering of faint freckles across her nose. "Let it go, Grant. I'm not going to date you."

His brow mimicked her earlier movement. "Because I'm not your type?"

"I do recall mentioning that only minutes ago." She shot visual daggers at him.

Fine. He wasn't so egotistical that he thought every woman wanted him. Only he knew Joni did. So why was she being so adamant that she didn't?

"What is your type?" he questioned, determined that if she wasn't going to date him he at least wanted to know her reasoning. "No one seems to know."

Her lips pursed. "Have you been checking up on me?"

He'd asked, put out feelers to make sure she wasn't involved with someone, to make sure she was free for him to ask out, to make sure no one raised red flags about her as a person. "Yeah, I guess I have, because I did ask around at the hospital."

She exhaled with an annoyed huff. "Great. Now everyone will know."

"Will know what?"

"That you asked about me." Her expression screamed, Duh!

His confidence was ebbing fast, as was his re-assurance at her sanity. "Is that a bad thing?"

"It's not a good thing." Her gaze shifted to the elevator button, then up at him expectantly.

Was he wrong? Had he imagined how this woman looked at him? How he caught her watching him? He'd bet his Hummer that she wanted him, too. So, why was she playing hard to get? Was there more going on than met the eye?

Grant didn't like games. Lord only knew, he'd played enough of those over the past few years with Ashley. But he liked Joni in a way that made him want to know more, that made him unwilling to let this go until he understood her rejection.

Which perhaps made him the world's biggest fool.

Because the right thing to do, what he should do, was lift his finger off the door-closed button, see her to her car, and forget about the pretty little nurse he thought about more often than not.

But that wasn't what he did.

Instead, he took advantage of how close they stood to each other in the elevator and, keeping one finger on the door closed button, with his free hand he lifted her chin.

"Fine. You don't want to date me. I'm not your type. Asking our co-workers about you prior to asking you out was a bad thing. But what about this?" he challenged.

She stared up at him with huge eyes. Her generous chest rose and fell in rapid, heavy breaths.

"If I kissed you, Joni, would that be a bad thing, too? Because I really want to kiss you and have wanted to for weeks. If that's not what you want, if you don't want me to kiss you, tell me to stop now."

Her pulse hammered at her throat. Her breath warmed his skin in fast little pants. She swallowed hard. Her lips parted as if she was going to speak, but not a word came out of her mouth. Instead, her eyelids closed, and a thousand emotions flashed across her lovely face all at once.

Ever so slightly her chin relaxed against his fingertips. Her lips parted another fraction. Her eyes remained tightly closed. Her breathing deepened.

She wasn't saying no. Her body language screamed, Yes. Oh, yes. He hadn't been wrong.

She wanted him to kiss her.

Which meant what? That she was playing hard to get? That she was stringing him along? Toying with him as Ashley had done?

He started to pull away, to cut his losses and put Joni out of his mind, or at least try since he hadn't had much luck up to that point. But her eyes opened and there was such vulnerability in their sea of green that he tumbled in.

Tumbled in and covered her mouth with his,

not one bit surprised at the immediate explosion of sensation weakening his knees.

The moment Grant's lips touched hers, Joni was lost.

Lost in wonder and excitement and awe.

His mouth brushed over hers with a feathery touch that was soft yet masterful. Gentle yet demanding. Hungry yet restrained. All Grant.

She didn't understand his interest in her, not really, but his kiss was so sweet, so tender, so hot that she couldn't pull away. Couldn't do anything except embrace the emotions flooding through her at the simple joy of his mouth conquering hers.

Of their own accord her fingers found their way into the golden brown waves of his hair, pulling his head closer to deepen the kiss. Her hand flattened against his cheek, loving the smoothness that was broken only by the hint of late evening stubble. Loving how his long, lean body pressed against her, so strong, so capable, so absolutely delicious.

And the way he smelled. Oh, my!

She inhaled deeply, dragging in his masculine scent the way she'd wanted to when she'd bumped into him earlier. Never had a man smelled better. Or tasted better. Never.

She wanted to fill her senses with him, to let his intoxicating presence drug her to all reality.

Which had her taking a dazed step back. Only there was no where to go because she already pushed into the hand railing. Panic clogged her throat, widened her eyes, stiffened her body.

What was she doing? She started to ask herself a thousand questions, but Grant's fingertip covered her lips. The gentle touch sent just as many shockwaves throughout her body as the taste of his lips had, as the feel of his strong body pressed against hers had, as the masculine musk of his scent had.

She wanted him. Right here, right now, in this elevator, she wanted him. That terrified her, made her feel out of control, something she'd sworn she'd never be again.

"Shh, don't."

Don't? her mind screamed. Wasn't it a little late for don't? They had.

Now she knew what she really needed not to know.

That he was everything that cocky smile promised.

That where Grant was concerned, she was going to have to up her guard or she was going to fall for him whether she wanted to or not.

That she might have thought he was like Mark, but she'd been wrong. Grant made Mark look like kid's play and the doctor she'd considered her future had tattered her heart and her whole life, almost pushed her into a well of despair that drowned her.

"Don't over-think what just happened. Just enjoy the moment." He flashed that lethal smile. The one that said he knew exactly what she was thinking, feeling, wanting, all of which involved him touching and kissing her a whole lot more. Enjoy the moment? Who was he kidding?

She geared up to blast him for having kissed her but before she made a single sound, she stopped.

How could she blast him? He hadn't forced her. No, he'd given her opportunity to stop him, and she hadn't. Instead, she'd closed her eyes and waited for him to kiss her.

Why hadn't she stopped him?

He ran his thumb along her jaw, leaving a tingly trail of awareness, reminding her exactly why she hadn't stopped him. Not that she'd known he had magic fingers, exactly, but chemistry had gotten the better of her.

"If not before, I'll see you Friday night."

She blinked, confusion adding to the mix of swirling emotions. "I'm not going out with you." At his fading smile, she rushed on, "I'm sorry if I misled you by not telling you not to kiss me. I should have, but I…" What could she say? That she'd been curious? Full of desire for him? That she had a mile-long masochistic streak and after five years of celibacy he made her want to throw caution to the wind with a single kiss? "But nothing's changed." Everything had changed. His kiss had turned her world upside down and inside out. She'd never look at him again without recalling how he'd curled her toes with his kiss. "I don't want to have a relationship with you outside our professional one at the hospital."

She really didn't want to have that one either. Too dangerous. She needed to stay far away from him. But unless she transferred out of the ICU, she'd have to deal with him on a regular basis. She loved working in ICU. She'd lost one job she loved because of a man, she wouldn't lose another.

"I know." But his eyes said otherwise, that her rejection confused him as much as he confused her. Probably just that he wondered how someone who was such a plain Jane would have the audacity to turn someone like him down. "I meant that I would see you at Hearts for Health on a non-date outing where we will both just happen to be," he pointed out, all apparent innocence.

"Oh." She searched his face for sarcasm, but only saw the ever-present twinkle in his eyes. The one that said he read minds and liked what she was thinking. He probably knew exactly the effect his kiss had had on her. Great.

He grinned and tweaked her nose. "Look, I'm sorry if I pushed more than I should have with the kiss, but I couldn't help myself. You have that effect on me." Another flash of the sexiest smile she'd ever seen. "I'll behave Friday night. Just give me a chance to get you past whatever makes you think you shouldn't go out with me. I promise I can change your mind."

He couldn't help himself? She had that effect on him? Hello, it wasn't as if she was the kind of woman to inspire men to lose all control. If she had been interested in dating, she'd be thrilled at the interest he was showing.

Who was she trying to kid? Deep down, she was thrilled at his interest. She was also terrified. A lot of years had passed since she'd been interested in a man, since she'd been touched, since she'd felt anything for the opposite sex.

Maybe too many years.

She had forgotten how good a man's touch felt.

Maybe she'd never known.

Had it felt that good when Mark had kissed her? Perhaps. She'd blocked the memories of her only lover for so long that she really couldn't recall how she'd felt the first time he'd touched her, kissed her. There was too much pain tied up in those memories to let them flood in now, so she shoved them back wherever they'd been hidden away.

As far as Grant changing her mind, well, that was what worried her. Based on her reaction to his kiss, he could change her mind all too easily, and then what? She'd be left with the fallout, left to pick up the pieces of her broken life. No, thank you. She was in charge of her destiny, not her libido.

"I probably won't even see you," she admitted slowly, not looking at him, not wanting him to see the fear coursing through her veins. Predators sensed fear and used it to their advantage, right? Yet thinking of him as a predator didn't quite fit. He had told her to tell him to stop if she didn't want his kiss. She had wanted him to kiss her. That was the problem. "I'm working the cake walk."

He grinned that smile that said he knew all and liked the power that came with it. She really should censor her thoughts around him—just in case.

"The cake walk? Imagine that. So am I." His eyes sparkling with mischief, he kissed the tip of her nose. "Who says you can't have your cake and eat it too?"

"How did you—?"

The elevator door slid open, interrupting her question.

Joni hadn't even realized he'd removed his finger from the button, hadn't even realized she was moving downward.

Had his kiss dazed her that much? Apparently.

She let him walk her to her car, let him open the door after she'd punched the unlock button on the key fob, let him close the door and watch her leave. All without another word.

All without admitting to herself that she hadn't "let" Grant do a darned thing. He was a man who took what he wanted one way or another. For some crazy reason he wanted her.

Holy water, garlic, and crucifixes warded off vampires, but what did one use when needing to ward off the devil himself? Especially when he kissed as sinfully deliciously as Grant?

Joni held her patient's hand while Grant pulled the tube free from the sixteen-year-old's chest.

Casts on his left arm and leg, both in traction, the young man grunted with his pain. He gritted his teeth, wanting to look tough in front of his parents, doctor, and nurse.

The boy had been in a car accident that had resulted in multiple fractures, crush injuries, and a collapsed lung. A surgeon had repaired a few internal bleeds and removed his spleen. An orthopedic surgeon had pinned his broken bones back together. Grant had been following the young man's pulmonary status from the point he'd been admitted to the ICU. If his lung didn't collapse again, he'd be transferred to the medical floor and sent home within a couple of days.

"You did great, Dale," Grant assured the boy, closing the wound as Joni handed Grant a pair of suture scissors. He ran through listening to the boy's lungs and assured himself there were breath sounds in all lung fields.

"Yes," the boy's mother praised, worry and fatigue from the past week's events obvious in her expression and body. "You're so brave."

"Right." Dale rolled his eyes, obviously embarrassed by her compliment.

Laughing, Grant patted the boy on the shoulder. "You are the man, Dale. Have your nurse page me if you get short of breath or have any negative change with your breathing."

He spoke with the boy for a few more minutes, then left the hospital room. The boy's parents followed him out, no doubt to corner him with questions.

Joni ran through another set of vital checks and made sure all the telemetry was still connected correctly. She reminded him what symptoms to watch for regarding his breathing, fractures, and other injuries, then left the room.

She wasn't surprised to find Grant in the hallway.

Distracted by the boy's parents, he seemed oblivious that she'd stepped out of the room. His navy scrubs hung loosely on his frame and he'd obviously raked his fingers through his hair a few times. Although barely seven a.m., he'd already been at the hospital for several hours, having gotten called in to the emergency room when a patient had gone into respiratory distress just prior to daybreak. No doubt he had an office full of patients waiting on him, too. Yet he answered each of the boy's parents' questions with admirable patience and a genuine smile.

He was a good doctor, gorgeous, kind, self-assured.

He'd kissed her.

She'd been fighting the thought from the moment she'd arrived at the hospital and learned he was already there.

No, truth was, she'd thought of nothing else the whole night. Even attending AA with her mother hadn't distracted her. When she'd finally drifted into sleep, she'd dreamed of him. Dreamed of his lips tasting hers, conquering, taking, mastering. When she'd wakened, she hadn't felt rested at all. She'd only felt restless, on edge, as if she'd been waiting for him, as if his kiss had awakened her and shot her to the precipice of the rest of her life.

Which was crazy.

She was no Sleeping Beauty and Grant was no Prince Charming. He had nothing to do with the rest of her life.

Once upon a time she'd believed in happily-ever-after. She'd been a wide-eyed innocent who'd believed the lies of a powerful man almost twice her age. Lies that had stolen her belief in fairy-tales, her self-respect, and had almost destroyed her life and career.

"Joni?"

She met Grant's gaze, saw the question in his eyes. She shook her head, sent a quick smile to the boys' parents, and went to check on another patient. A twenty-two-year-old who'd been in an MVA two nights before and had yet to regain consciousness.

"You okay?"

Not having realized that he'd followed her into the patient's room, she spun, startled.

"Sorry, I didn't mean to scare you." His fingers brushed over her arm, eliciting thousands of goose-bumps.

Why was he always touching her?

"You don't scare me."

His lips twisted. "Actually, I think I do."

"Oh, get over yourself. Not every woman wants you." Clamping her lips closed, she cast a quick glance at her unconscious patient. She wanted the boy to wake up, to give her a reason to move away from Grant. A reason that he couldn't mistake as fear.

"True," he admitted. "But we're not talking about every woman, are we? We're talking about you."

She glared, not liking him.

"Whether you're willing to admit it or not, you do want me, Joni." He smiled that smile that was really starting to get on her nerves. "And for reasons I don't understand yet, I definitely scare you."

CHAPTER THREE

"SO WHAT'S up with you and Dr. Take My Breath Away?"

Joni pretended not to hear Samantha's question, just set down the box of cakes she'd made for the cake walk on the long table in the community room.

"Hello." Samantha snapped her fingers in front of Joni's face. "The man asked me all kinds of questions about you right down to where I thought he was going to have me sign an affidavit stating I was telling the truth, the whole truth, and nothing but the truth, so help me God. I've seen how you two look at each other and thought there was something there, but you never said anything so I thought maybe you just didn't realize yet. Then he walked you to your car the other night and you've been tighter than a clam ever since. Best friend here." She thumped her chest. "I want details. Lotsa details."

Taking a red velvet cake out of the box, Joni found an empty spot on the table, then turned to her friend. "What makes you think there are lotsa details?"

"The fact that you're being so evasive and blushing like the entire football team just saw you in your undies."

"Well, it is a little warm in here." She made a pretense of fanning her face.

"Right." Samantha shivered and glanced around the mostly vacant community room. "I expect to see a group of penguins and a few polar bears go strolling by any moment there's such a heat wave in this place. Brrrr."

Okay, so her friend had a point. Due to expecting such a crowd, the thermostat had been set low to cool the building off prior to hundreds of warm bodies heating up the place.

Joni finished emptying the box and stooped to slide the box beneath the table. "You going to help me set up the cake walk?"

"I thought that was my job."

Grant!

Samantha gave her a "you are so going to tell me everything later" look. "Yeah, I'm pretty sure it is. Besides, I'm needed at the ticket table. A lot of work setting that up, you know."

"You need us to help you?" Grant offered, carefully putting the box he held on an empty spot on the table.

"I've got it covered." Samantha shook her head, made eye contact with Joni and did an "I'm watching you" finger motion before leaving the community room to head towards the front of the building where tickets would be sold.

"This doesn't start for almost an hour, you know," Joni pointed out as she watched her friend bail on her for the second time that week. Some best friend.

"I know. I came to help with set-up." He pulled out several home-made cakes that had Joni's mouth watering. Wow. How many little old ladies had he hit up for that stash?

She eyed him suspiciously. "Did you know I was helping with set-up?"

Not looking one bit ashamed, he grinned. "Would you believe a little birdie told me?"

"Ha. I'd believe a big birdie told you." Her gaze went toward where Samantha had just disappeared through the double doors.

He laughed. "I can't let Samantha take the blame for this one. Brooke in Admissions told me."

"Brooke?" Joni shook her head. Just how many of her friends had he talked to? "Do I have no friends?"

"Oh, you have lots of friends. They all think you are a great nurse, a great person, although a bit of a control freak. You like your privacy and have no romantic life that any of them are aware of."

Joni's jaw dropped. "They told you all that?"

"What can I say? Apparently, they like me."

Good thing she didn't have enemies.

"They don't know you like I do," she quipped.

"True," he admitted, taking the last of the cakes out of the box and arranging it just so on the table. "And you don't know me anywhere near as well as you're going to. Now, where do we start?"

Joni started to argue with him that she didn't want to know him better, but what was the point? He would just flash that smile of his and keep right on going.

"Fine," she acquiesced, just ready to get this enforced time with him done and over with. "Carry this box over to the middle of that section and we'll lay out our cake-walk squares. I checked earlier and all twenty-four squares are there. We just have to get them laid out in an eye-pleasing way."

"Eye-pleasing, eh?"

"Grant—"

"I know, I know, get to work. Such a control-freak slave-driver." He picked up the box and began doing her bidding one cake-walk square at a time while she pretended not to notice how his jeans hugged his behind and thighs in a way that made her want to moan.

Great. Just shoot her now, because tonight was going to be a long, torturous night.

Punching the Play button on the old-fashioned boombox being used for the cake walk's sound system, Grant grinned at his cute assistant who held the container full of numbered cards.

Apparently loving the festivities, Joni had been smiling all evening. Well, all except for when she looked directly at him.

Then she frowned. But only a few times since he'd first arrived and caught her off guard. Good, he liked catching her off guard because then she didn't have time to slide that masked expression into place.

Not that she'd masked her expression much tonight.

Whether she wanted to admit it or not, she was having fun. A lot of fun. With him.

So was he. With her.

How long since he'd felt this attracted to a woman? This relaxed? Years, thanks to Ashley. Why had he let her take over his life so? Well, he knew why. Staying with her had been easier than dealing with the drama of breaking up.

But sometimes love wasn't enough. In Ashley's case that had held true. Or maybe he hadn't been enough. Definitely not enough to keep her away from the demons that drove her.

Grant pulled his mind back to the present, determined not to let the past drag him down, not tonight. Not ever again. He'd moved to Bean's Creek to make a new start. He'd needed to make a fresh start. He had, right down to meeting Joni and knowing he wanted more than just a co-worker relationship with her. Knowing he wanted more than just friendship with her but proceeding with caution because he didn't want to end up right back in a similar relationship he'd been in with Ashley.

What he wanted was to peel off those snug jeans and kiss his way down the curve of Joni's hips, the lushness of her thighs, the tonedness of her calves, right down to the arch of her foot. Was she ticklish? Would she squirm free from his embrace, giggling and retaliating with touches and kisses of her own? Or would she simply moan in pleasure?

He closed his eyes, swallowed. Hard. If he didn't get his mind on the job at hand and off Joni, he was going to be hard. He was about halfway there already. More than halfway.

"Grant?"

His gaze went to Joni's expectant one. She was so beautiful, so full of verve, so tempting. "Hmm?"

Brows drawn tight, she gave him a pointed look. "Don't you think the music has gone long enough this round?"

Grant grimaced. He'd forgotten to stop the music. The cake walkers had been circling around the numbered squares for God only knew how long. He covered his slip with a grin. "I was building the suspense."

"It's built." She sounded breathy, and his gaze dropped to where her sweater hugged her full chest. Never in his life had he been jealous of a shirt, but tonight he'd like to be wrapped around Joni. When he'd first arrived, the room had been cold and she'd been at high attention, had captured his notice and his imagination. Flashes of sliding his hands beneath her sweater, tweaking those taunt peaks, cupping those generous breasts, had been teasing him all evening.

"And," she continued, oblivious to how he wanted to drag her beneath the table full of cakes and nibble his way around her body, "Mrs. Lehew is about to need to replace her portable oxygen tank if she has to make another lap."

If he kept staring at Joni's tight little sweater, he was going to need portable oxygen himself.

"You might be right." He pressed the button to pause the music, pointed to the basket of numbered cards for Joni to draw out a winner. "Have at it."

"Number eleven," she called, casting him another odd look, before smiling sweetly at the seven—or eight-year-old snaggle-toothed boy who was jumping up and down on the number eleven block. Instantly, Grant had visions of Joni jumping up and down on the square, of her sweater outlining her breasts as they bounced and jiggled and beckoned to him. His jeans grew tighter. Too tight. Any moment he was going to lose all circulation in the lower half of his body.

Immediately after the young boy claimed his prize, Joni called for the crowd's attention, again. "Since Dr. Bradley got a little carried away by the music..." she sent him a sugary smile "...stay on your squares, because we're going to pick another winner." She reached into the basket and pulled out another card. "Number fourteen."

"Mrs. Lehew." Despite his uncomfortable jeans, Grant laughed. "You sure you didn't rig that win, Nurse Joni?"

At her impish grin, he realized she'd done exactly that.

"Call it preventative medicine because the poor woman really can't manage any more trips around the cake walk. I didn't know how she was going to manage to begin with, but then you made her go even longer despite the fact she was slowing down the entire procession."

He really hadn't picked a good time to zone out with thoughts about Joni and leave the cake walkers going round and round. But the smile on Mrs Lehew's face said if she'd minded in the slightest, she no longer did.

"Maybe since she won a cake she'll sit out the remaining walks because if not," Joni mused, "we're going to have to find a designated walker for her."

"Or a wheelchair."

The ecstatic obese woman with severe chronic

obstructive pulmonary disease excitedly took Joni's hand. "Oh, thank you. Thank you. I can't believe this. I never win."

"Well, you did tonight. Congratulations. Here's your cake, Mrs. Lehew." She handed the woman a chocolate-frosted cake from the long table still loaded with donated goodies.

"You know," Grant mused, scratching his chin with a feigned thoughtful look, "it's a good thing I'm her pulmonologist and not her endocrinologist or I'd have to protest that cake."

"Good thing," Joni agreed, responding to his teasing with a slight lifting of her mouth at the corners. "Then again, maybe she wanted to win the cake for her grandchildren or maybe she just wanted to do the cake walk to support a really good cause."

"We can tell ourselves that."

Joni's lips twitched. "But you're not buying it?"

"Not after her last hospital admission and seeing how well controlled her sugar was when she didn't have easy access to snacks and junk food."

Looking as if she might tackle the elderly

woman and wrestle the cake from her, Joni glanced toward Mrs. Lehew.

Sorry he'd mentioned the woman's uncontrolled diabetes, Grant touched Joni's hand. "It's okay. I learned a long time ago that you can't control what others do to themselves. You can only encourage them to do the right thing and hope they are paying attention." So maybe saying he'd learned that lesson a long time ago was stretching the truth, but he had learned. Eventually. "If she wants cake, she's going to have cake regardless of whether or not she wins one here." He squeezed Joni's hand, wanting to see her face light up with a smile again, wanting the sense of camaraderie, albeit precarious, they'd shared while doling out cakes to continue. "Besides, that one is for her grandkids."

Nodding resignedly, Joni gave him what appeared to be an appreciative smile. "Sure it is. If she ends up in the emergency room tonight with a five hundred blood sugar, I'm going to feel as if I put her there."

"No need for that. Look." Grant gestured in the direction the woman had headed and Joni's gaze followed suit. Mrs. Lehew was sitting at a table with three small children clamoring to get a better look at her prize. They were calling her Granny and tugging on her sleeves.

"Oh, you're good," she praised with a hint of sarcasm.

"I know." When Joni's gaze met his, he winked. "Oh, you meant because of Mrs. Lehew? What? You mean you didn't believe me?" He tsked. "Shame. Shame."

But rather than correct him or slap him down, she just gave a resigned sigh and turned back to the cake walkers.

They collected the tickets from the next group in line, then Grant restarted the music and turned to her.

"You'll find that I am many things, Joni, but you can take what I tell you to the bank."

"Meaning?"

"Meaning that when I tell you how I've thought of little else except kissing you again, that I want to kiss you again, you can believe it's the truth."

"I don't doubt that you want to kiss me again."

She didn't sound happy about the prospect,

though. Not exactly the reaction he'd hoped for. He wanted her to quit fighting the attraction between them and admit she wanted him too. He wanted whatever had her running scared to fade into the background and for her to embrace the chemistry between them. Still, she wasn't saying no.

"That confident that you were that good?" he teased.

"No, you are the one who just commented about how good you are, remember?" She shook the basket of numbered cards. "I'm just that confident that you see me as a challenge, and that's why you're so determined to pursue me," she countered. "But I'm not a challenge, Grant. I'm a real person with real feelings. I don't want to be hurt."

Grant started to speak, but she leaned over and punched the Pause button, killing the music and effectively drawing all eyes to them. Without another glance his way, she pulled out a card. "Number nineteen."

Why did Grant keep looking at her as if he wanted to peel off her clothes and take a bite?

Joni bit the inside of her lip, wondering if she was going to gnaw a hole right through if she didn't stay away from a certain doctor. She'd accused him of seeing her as a challenge because that was what her brain had decided was the logical conclusion. Was that why he kept coming back for more of her pushing him away?

No, truth was, she was beginning to think he really liked her. The more she thought about it, the more likable he was, too. For all his cockiness, he was just as likely to say something self-deprecating to make her smile. Why, oh, why, did he have to be so likeable on top of how completely hunky he was? After all, she was only a mortal woman. How was she supposed to resist his allure when everything about him appealed?

She did her best to ignore him for the rest of their cake-walk stint. Not an easy thing when they were working to keep the cake walk going, but she did manage to avoid any more private talk.

A few minutes prior to the end, Vann and Samantha got into the cakewalk line.

"If I don't win, you are in so-o-o much trouble," Samantha teased, handing Joni her ticket and casting a questioning gaze toward Grant. She gave Joni two thumbs-ups. Puh-leeze. Even her best friend was matchmaking. Spare her.

Besides, she was irked at Samantha for bailing twice. And for telling Grant no telling what.

Ignoring Samantha's go-for-it sign, Joni shrugged. "Sorry, sugarplum." She never used endearments so this got a giggle out of her friend. "But your odds are the same as everyone else's. One out of twenty-four."

"I'll take those odds. Especially since Vann bought our tickets." Samantha patted his arm, keeping her hand on his biceps. Her friend usually insisted on paying her equal share, so the fact she'd let Vann pay was significant. Vann didn't look impressed. Actually, he looked irked, too.

Joni shot a curious gaze back and forth between the two, but Samantha just borrowed one from Joni's book and shrugged.

"Hey, Vann, you expecting special favors, too?" Joni asked, giving her friendliest smile and hoping to ease whatever strain was in the air.

Stepping out of Samantha's hold, he nodded.

"Samantha wants cake, so let her eat cake. Lord forbid, she doesn't get everything she wants right when she wants it. To hell with the rest of the world."

Joni forced a laugh at his quip, hoping to ease the tension jetting back and forth between her two dear friends. Unfortunately, Samantha was now glaring at her boyfriend. Surely he hadn't proposed again tonight? Vann proposals were always followed by a fight, which was usually followed by making up and then another few months of the status quo before they repeated the process all over again. Eventually, Vann was going to tire of Samantha's refusals. But, for now, apparently he was hopeful enough that he'd change her mind to keep sticking it out. Either that or he liked their make-up ritual.

As far as Joni was concerned, Dr. Vann Winton was the sole good guy left in the world. Then again, he was a cardiologist so maybe he naturally had more heart.

Having finished collecting the rest of the tickets, Grant joined them.

"Vann." Samantha stepped forward. "This is

Dr. Bradley, the pulmonologist I was telling you about. He's a miracle worker in the ICU. I've seen him yank patients back from the other side on more than one occasion. I swear he must have made a pact with God somewhere along the way." Then she waggled her brows and said a bit too brightly, "Or with the someone who hails from down below. Pun intended."

Joni couldn't argue Samantha's point. Hadn't she often wondered if Grant was really the devil himself?

Vann eyed Grant warily, making Joni question just what her friend had said about Grant in private. Still, polite as always, he stuck out his hand. "Dr. Vann Winton. I practice in Winston-Salem. Nice to meet you."

Grant whistled. "I've heard of you. I enjoyed that article you wrote about the promising beneficial effects of Tracynta on the treatment of pulmonary hypertension."

Vann's expression changed and if they'd had time, the two men would have launched into a conversation about whatever the article had said. Interesting. Vann usually took a while to warm up to strangers, but with one comment Grant had won him over to the dark side. Joni almost sighed. Maybe the man's appeal wasn't limited to little old ladies and nurses.

Samantha and Vann took their places on the numbered squares. Using the microphone, Grant briefly explained the rules to this round's walkers. When Joni called out the winning number, Samantha didn't win.

Vann did.

His lips curved in a smile. With wry amusement, he handed the cake over to an ecstatic Samantha, then he looked at Joni. "What did I tell you? If she wants cake, I give the woman cake."

Samantha leaned forward, whispered something in his ear that only he could hear.

His face brightened further, turning his already handsome face into a thing of beauty. "Apparently, I'm going to thoroughly enjoy her having her cake, too."

Giggling, Samantha nodded. "Oh, yeah, you're going to enjoy my…cake."

"I've heard of enjoying pie…" Grant mused,

feigning innocence and making Samantha laugh again. Joni just rolled her eyes at them all.

Leaning close, Vann and Samantha obviously were no longer aware that anyone existed other than the two of them.

Unexpected envy shot through Joni. Which didn't make sense. She was happy. She had a great life.

Active, healthy, a sober mother, a job where she made a difference in people's lives. She had the life she had chosen for herself, that she had worked hard to make happen, and she wouldn't let anything, or anyone, threaten it. But when Vann's hand settled low on Samantha's back in a purely possessive move, Joni felt an ache. An ache that something major was missing.

Not that she needed a man to be happy. She didn't. But maybe she'd discounted the benefits of physical contact with an attractive person. Maybe she'd miscalculated when she'd buried herself so effectively behind her protective walls five years ago. Maybe life wasn't so cut and dried.

Maybe she could have her cake and eat it too.

Or at least have a lick of icing every now and again.

Really, she'd let Mark steal much more from her than she'd realized. Let her focus remain on keeping her mother sober to the exclusion of her own life.

She wanted cake.

Beef cake, a perverse little voice taunted from somewhere in her head. Yes, she wanted beef-cake.

She wanted Grant.

After Mark she'd promised herself she'd never get involved with another doctor, that she'd never get involved with another playboy, period, no matter what his profession.

In reality, she hadn't gotten involved with any-one.

Not since she'd been a nursing student who'd fallen for a man in power who'd been so brilliant, so suave, so exciting to be around that she'd given him her heart and her body.

In the end, he'd burned her so badly she had only existed for months. For years.

She wanted to do more than exist.

She wanted to live.

Life at its fullest stood just a few feet away, tempting her with the sweetest pleasures. Only... could she?

If he only saw her as a challenge, should she? But how would she know if she just sat on the sidelines of life?

She wanted to know. She wanted Grant. And cake.

Heat fusing through her, Joni's gaze met his. Tension sparked. Was he thinking the same thing she was? Was he envisioning them sharing cake? Her spreading the whipped icing on that marvelous chest of his and licking it off one trace of her tongue over his skin at a time?

When his eyes lowered, settled onto her lips, visions erupted of him feeding her icing off his fingertip and then kissing her to share in the sweetness.

Oh, my. Her breath caught in her throat and she forcibly sucked in a deep breath to stay conscious.

Every cell in her body tingled, cried out for cake.

Her lips parted, then curved into a smile.

If she went in knowing she and Grant were just about chemistry, if she was the one who made the rules and Grant was willing to play by them, why couldn't she have cake?

CHAPTER FOUR

GRANT watched the slideshow of emotions flicker over Joni's face. God, she was beautiful. And tortured. And everything he wanted.

Or maybe she was just intent on torturing him because she was the only thing he wanted?

But despite the heat that burned, she insisted upon keeping those walls between them. Walls so high he wondered if he was ever going to scale them.

So when her expression softened, her lips parted, and her pupils dilated with what appeared to be lust, he took a step back from shock.

Then she smiled.

Full fledged, full force, Joni smiled. At him.

Grant wanted to tell the cake walkers to get lost, that he was going to push Joni down on those numbered squares and feast on the most divine woman's lips, that he was going to help himself to one of the cakes and smear icing on her throat and sup the sticky sweetness off one delectable sup at a time. He'd search out all her sensitive spots and repeat the process until she arched into his touch, until she offered him the sugary goodness of her body, shaming the sweetest of confections.

On cue, their replacements arrived and without a word Grant handed the microphone to Jamie, a phlebotomist he'd seen around the hospital a few times. Taking the basket of numbers from Joni, he handed them to, hell, he had no idea who he handed them to, just that he shoved them towards someone and someone took them.

What he knew was that when he grabbed Joni's hand, her skin was soft and warm against his. Her hand felt right. So right. More importantly, she didn't pull away.

Instead, she squeezed his hand, laced her fingers with his, kept up with him as he wove them out of the room full of people. He didn't pause when spoken to, just nodded an acknowledgement and kept heading toward the door, intent on finding someplace private so he could devour the woman next to him. Escape was only a few feet away when Dr. Abellano, the hospital's medical director, patted him on the shoulder.

"Grant." The man's voice sounded remarkably like Sean Connery's. "There's someone I'd like you to meet."

Would it be rude to say he didn't want to meet anyone? That all he wanted was to get Joni somewhere where they could be alone? His gaze shot to her. He knew his exasperation showed, but she just smiled at him. A knowing little smile that said she wanted out of this room as much as he did.

This had better not take long, otherwise he might be looking for a new job in the near future for ditching the medical director so he could go have his way with an ICU nurse.

"Hello, Dr. Abellano." He managed to hide his impatience.

The man nodded a brief acknowledgement to Joni, then redirected his attention to Grant. He kept talking, but Grant was only catching bits of the man's words. How could he focus on the older gentleman when Joni's pink tongue darted out and licked the corner of her mouth?

Unbelievably, she was teasing him, torturing him in a whole new way. She knew he hadn't wanted to stop, that he was having trouble focusing on what his boss was saying. He buried a growl deep in his chest, wanting to bury himself deep inside her instead. Didn't she know how desperately he wanted to strip off those jeans and sweater, push her against the wall, and make her scream his name?

Actually, he was pretty sure she did know and that she was enjoying herself. Which just made him want to strip her naked and make her enjoy herself all the more in other, more physical ways. To make her lose that tight control she clung to.

No, he needed to slow down, get a handle on the lust surging through him. For their first time he didn't want it to be rushed against a wall. He wanted a big bed and a bunch of hours to prove to her how good a relationship could be between them.

There would be a first time.

Whether tonight or next week or next month,

there would be a first time between them. Dozens more. Hundreds even. If ever he had doubted the chemistry between them, staring into her eyes, he no longer did. He saw the stars, the moon, the promise of all the heavens above staring back at him in her green eyes. He wanted every out-of-this world experience she offered and to give them back to her tenfold.

"This is my daughter, Heather," Dr. Abellano introduced.

Grant barely glanced at the woman, greeted her only to keep from being discourteous to his boss and in the hope of quelling his libido enough to take a slow hand with Joni. But when Joni's gaze settled on the woman, her smile disappeared so quickly Grant took another look.

Heather Abellano was an extraordinarily beautiful woman. Tall, statuesque, dark, wavy hair, and almond-shaped brown eyes that popped. But she wasn't the woman whose hand he held. Neither was she the woman he desperately wanted to be alone with.

"Heather is a cardiologist just finishing up residency. She will be at the hospital for a few weeks." The medical director couldn't have sounded more like a proud father if he'd tried. "Make her feel welcome, won't you?"

The newcomer stuck out her hand. Hating to let go of Joni's hand, Grant did and exchanged quick pleasantries with the woman.

When he turned to introduce Joni, she was gone.

Joni slid into the seat next to Samantha, set her barbecue plate on the table, and took a big gulp of her diet soda.

Anything to quell the burn in her throat. Not that the rather flat soda was helping.

"So, what was that all about?" Samantha asked before the liquid even hit Joni's churning stomach.

She met her friend's gaze. "You tell me. Are you and Vann fighting?"

Taking a deep breath, Samantha shook her head. "Earlier, but not any more."

Joni popped a potato chip into her mouth, soaking up the salty goodness on her tongue. "He proposed again, didn't he?"

"At the front ticket desk." Samantha stuck her finger in her throat and made a gagging noise. "He walked up to the table where I sat with Bobbie Jean Evans and he asked me to marry him. How unromantic is that?"

Considering the man had already proposed a dozen times and had just driven in from Winston-Salem, Joni imagined that mustering romance knowing one was likely to be rejected yet again might be difficult. At least Vann was persistent.

What her friend had said hit her.

"Do you want romance?" Had she been misreading Samantha all this time? She'd thought, like her, Samantha didn't believe in happily ever after, but maybe her friend wanted the fairy-tale.

"Of course I want romance," Samantha confirmed, blowing Joni's mind a little. "What woman doesn't want romance?"

It might not be a good time to raise her hand. Especially in light of the fact that she so didn't want the conversation turning back to her and Grant. Not that there had been anything romantic between them, only…no, that had just been chemistry. Chemistry got people into trouble, got her into trouble. Much better to focus on her best friend's love life than her own.

"Does Vann know you want romance?" she asked, popping another chip into her mouth.

"He should. I've told him often enough."

She considered her friend's answer. "But does he know? I mean, really know that's what you want from him?"

Because Joni believed there wasn't much the man wouldn't do to convince Samantha to walk down the aisle.

"I don't know how he couldn't know. I've practically beat him over the head with it. Sometimes I think we've dated too long, we're too comfortable with each other, and that we'd be better off just being friends." She dropped her head to the table and beat her forehead against the molded plastic a couple of times. "Only he's all I've ever known, and I can't imagine my life without him."

Joni tried to imagine what it would have been like if she'd had a Vann, a man who'd been a part of her life from adolescence into womanhood, a man who'd brought her into womanhood, a man who'd held her hand during the hard times rather than turn on her. Yeah, she supposed the idea of letting that safety net go would be terrifying. Especially when that safety net was a man as wonderful as Vann. Still, he was obviously missing the clues her friend was dropping.

"Men can be so dense." Such as the fact she'd been ready to throw caution to the wind with Grant and he'd become distracted by a luscious brunette cardiologist.

"Such as Dr. Bradley?" Samantha echoed her thoughts. "Is he dense?"

"As a brick." Did the man have attention deficit disorder or what? For weeks now he'd been setting the stage to ask her out, had asked her out for this very night. The exact minute she'd decided to give in to the pull between them, he'd gone googly-eyed over another woman. Maybe she'd been dead on the money when she'd decided he just saw her as a challenge. Once she'd mentally acquiesced, she'd lost all appeal.

"A brick, eh?" Samantha laughed, then took a bite of her sandwich. "So, tell me what he did," she said between chews.

"He didn't do anything." Not really. She supposed he'd only been polite. Yet seeing his gaze rake over the brunette had ripped off a scab to a wound she hadn't wanted opened, to a wound that ran deep and left her raw even years later.

"The man walked you to your car the other night, practically whisked you away from the cake walk, and you're telling me he didn't do anything either time? Not even a kiss?" Samantha's gaze narrowed as if that would give her the power to see right into Joni's head. "Right. I believe that. So, where have you been for the past fifteen minutes?"

"You should believe me. It's true." Joni forked a big bite of meat and poked the whole thing in her mouth. The spicy flavor made her mouth water. "I've been in the bathroom, trying to figure out what I want from Grant."

"The bathroom? What you want from Grant?" Samantha stared at her a moment, pushed her plate back, and turned in her chair to fully face Joni. "Tell me what happened back there."

Vann chose that moment to return to the table and put Samantha's drink in front of her. Samantha pointed towards the table of drinks. A line had formed of folks ordering. "Go get Joni a sweet tea, please."

Glancing back and forth between the two women, he nodded and went to find sweet tea.

"Forget romance. You really should marry him, you know," Joni said between bites. "He's a great catch."

"So am I," Samantha countered without skipping a beat. "You really should tell me what happened between you and Dr. Make Me Breathe Hard a few minutes ago, you know."

"That's an easy one. Nothing happened." Which was the truth because Samantha had asked about a few minutes ago and not about an elevator kiss that had poisoned her mind to all else.

No wonder she'd given in to the silly idea that she could have her cake and eat it too. Grant's kiss had infected her mind.

"But something is going to happen between you, isn't it?"

Was it? Joni sighed. "No." Pause. "Maybe." Another pause. "I think so."

"You think so? Woman, that man is hot and he was looking at you as if he wanted to spread his icing all over your cake, so to speak."

Leave it to Samantha to say something so outlandish, so totally inappropriate, yet that somehow worked. Sticking another potato chip in her mouth, Joni sought the right words to explain to her friend. "There's this thing between us. I don't understand, but it's definitely there."

"It's called chemistry, baby."

Ignoring that her friend had interrupted, Joni went on, "There's this chemistry between us. I don't understand it or even want it, but its there all the same."

"So what are you going to do about it?"

"That's what I spent fifteen minutes in the bathroom trying to figure out."

Samantha stared expectantly. "And?"

"Maybe I'm not going to do anything."

"Maybe you should."

"I…well, there for a minute I thought maybe, but now…"

"But now what? A gorgeous man is attracted to you and guess what? You're attracted to him, too. What could be a more perfect scenario? Life is short. Live a little. Smile. Laugh. Have some fun."

Samantha made it sound so simple. Just two people being attracted to each other and…and then what exactly? What was she so afraid of? "I don't want to get hurt."

Samantha placed her hand on Joni's. "That I understand."

"Vann would never hurt you."

"Not intentionally." She glanced up and smiled at the man they spoke of and who had just re-joined them.

"Thank you," Joni said when he gave her the disposable plastic cup of sweet iced tea.

"I hope you don't mind…" Vann took his seat across from them and pulled his plate toward him "…but I invited Dr. Bradley to join our table."

"Goodie," Samantha said, rubbing her palms together and earning a confused frown from Vann.

Joni was going to elbow her friend, but Grant stepped up to the table, a plate loaded with food in one hand and a drink in the other. "Hope I'm not intruding."

Ha, right. Would he leave if she told him he was?

"Of course you're not," Samantha assured him, gesturing to the empty seat across from Joni. "Have a seat."

"What happened to your new friend?" Joni could have bit her wayward tongue the second the question slipped out.

His brow arched. "Dr. Abellano's daughter?"

"Is that who she was?" Oh, she didn't sound jealous at all. Not one bit. Great. She couldn't look at Samantha because she was pretty sure that if she did her friend would burst out laughing.

"If you'd stuck around you would know that's who she was because I was going to introduce you but you disappeared. And I have no idea where she is now," he said, sliding into the seat next to her rather than into the empty seat next to Vann, leaving Vann alone on the opposite side of the table. "You jealous?" he asked close to her ear.

"Ha." She feigned indifference, wondering if she was really that easy for the world to read. "Why would I be jealous?"

Why was her face on fire?

"Why indeed?" He grinned, obviously liking the pink tinge to her cheeks.

She was not jealous.

Was she? Yet when she analyzed her reaction, she had been jealous. Very jealous. Great. She hadn't even gone out on a single date with the man and yet she felt possessive about him? Not good. Not good at all. Maybe Dr. Abellano had done her a favor by interrupting, reminding her of another man she'd been attracted to, another man who had led her down a treacherous path. Yes, she owed the beautiful cardiologist a thank you. Obviously, she'd lost her mind there for a few minutes, thinking it would be okay to become involved with a man like Grant.

Being involved with Grant would be like playing Russian roulette. With a fully loaded gun and the devil egging her on.

But she wasn't a coward, was she? As uncomfortable as Grant made her feel, a part of her liked how alive he made her feel.

As long as she didn't fall in love with him, didn't risk her career, what would giving in to chemistry hurt? It wasn't as if she thought there would ever be anything more between them than physical attraction. She didn't even want there to be anything more between them. Actually, she didn't want that either, but apparently her body hadn't gotten the memo.

"You have no reason to be jealous of Heather Abellano or any other woman."

Any moment her cheeks were going to burst into flames. "I realize that."

Of course, she didn't have any rights where he was concerned. So he'd asked her out, told her he wanted her, had looked at her as if he wanted to wallow in cake icing with her. That didn't mean she owned him. She knew that. He could be with anyone he wanted and she had no right to say a single word of protest.

"That's not what I meant." He quickly interrupted her thoughts, giving her an exasperated look. "You always jump to the wrong conclusions where I'm concerned, Joni. Give me a little credit. I meant that from the moment I first saw you I haven't been interested in any woman except you."

Her gaze shot to his.

"Just you," he emphasized.

Grant's words released a thousand butterflies in her stomach at once, made her feel light-headed, and threw her completely off kilter. She hadn't expected his claim. Although perhaps she should have. He constantly threw curve balls her way.

Okay, so, try as she might, resisting the man was futile. He really was the devil in handsome-doctor disguise.

She liked him, was attracted to him, wanted him to touch and kiss her, emotions she hadn't felt since Mark.

"I want you." His words came out a caress, wrapping around her with warmth and desire, drawing her in and making her want to lean toward him. "I want you a lot."

She wanted him a lot, too.

"Why?" she asked, wondering if she should elbow Samantha for eavesdropping because her friend's curiosity coated her as palpably as a blanket. Or maybe that was Samantha's breath on her back from where her friend leaned in so close?

"Honestly?" He shrugged. Taking a bite of his barbecue sandwich, he considered her question. "I don't know. There was something about you that caught my eye from the beginning and made me want to get to know you. I'm not sure how to label that. I just know I haven't been able to stop thinking about you since we met."

"Because you want to have sex with me?" She was pretty sure she'd shocked herself as much as she had him with her bold question. Based on Samantha's gasp, she'd definitely shocked her friend. Good, maybe it was time to shake up her life. No more just existing. No more vanilla. She wanted wild raspberry swirl or some other exotic flavor, even if only a brief lick.

Even if only while playing by a cautious set of rules meant to keep everything tidy and neat, controlled.

Grant's blue gaze met hers. "That's a trick question, Joni. If I say no then that implies I don't want to have sex with you. That would be a lie because we both know I want you in my bed." He paused and gave her a sexy grin. "And in your bed and about a dozen other places."

Joni swallowed, closed her eyes at the images flashing through her mind at his words. Only the jab of Samantha's finger into her back kept her from leaning over and telling Grant to take her to any of those places this very minute. All of those places. Over and over.

"But if I say yes," he continued in a way-too-logical tone of voice, "then it makes me look like a cad just out to bag another babe."

"That's not what this is about?"

He pushed his barely touched plate back and turned to fully face her. "I don't know exactly what this is about. But I would like the opportunity to find out. With the exception of in the elevator, you've shot me down at every turn."

"I don't want to be used. Or hurt. Or made a fool."

"Neither do I."

His softly spoken words sounded so sincere, so heartfelt that Joni reeled. Had he been used in the past? Had someone hurt him as much as Mark had hurt her? Why did that thought make her want to wrap her arms around him and hold him tight? Despite whatever this connection they shared was, she barely knew the man. She shouldn't want to comfort him. No way.

Yet she did.

"I'm not sure what to say," she finally admitted.

"You say, 'My place or yours?'" Samantha advised from beside Joni. "And what the heck happened in the elevator and why haven't I heard all the juicy details?"

Grant grinned at Samantha's advice. Joni rolled her eyes, then shook her head as she found herself smiling, too.

"I have some bids in on the raffles." Where that inane comment came from Joni had no idea. She did have bids in at the raffle but, hello, winning a basketful of gardening supplies or bath and beauty products wasn't the be-all and end-all. Not when the most gorgeous man she'd ever met was telling her that he wanted her in his bed.

"Bids? Seriously?" Samantha elbowed her, echoing her thoughts. "There is no basket here that offers what you need."

It had been a long time since she'd let a man close to her, physically or otherwise. How did she even know what she needed? What she wanted? Grant confused her.

She wanted him. Denying it wouldn't make it less true.

Try as she might to fight the way he affected her, she would be having an affair. But she wasn't a fool. Not any more. Not ever again. If she was going to do this, they'd do so on her terms, by her rules, when she was ready.

Elbowing Samantha, hopefully into silence, she twisted in her seat to where her back was completely to Samantha. She met Grant's amused expression. "When we're through eating, perhaps you'd join my nosy friend and I during the auction and raffle?"

"I heard that," Samantha said from behind her.

"I'd like that," he agreed, giving her the smile that would have Mrs. Sain's heart monitor beep-beep-beeping.

Joni's heart was doing a beep-beep-beeping of

its own, but she didn't look away from the intensity in Grant's eyes. Instead she gave what she hoped was a mysterious smile of her own and said, "Me, too."

Grant couldn't drag his gaze away from Joni during the charity auction. Not when she excitedly bid on a spa package, only to lose when the cost ran up beyond what she was willing to pay. Or when she burst out laughing when she won a free eight-by-ten photo during the raffle draw.

"As if I want an eight-by-ten photo of myself."

Grant couldn't help but think he wouldn't mind an eight-by-ten picture of Joni. Although no photo could ever capture the essence of the woman beside him.

He'd seen her relaxed with patients and with her co-workers, but never had she been relaxed around him. Until tonight. Something had changed in her mindset while they'd been eating their barbecue dinner. Something that had put a predatory gleam in her eyes whenever she looked at him.

Not that she needed a predatory gleam when it came to him.

He was more than willing to play mouse to her cat just so long as he got to play with her.

The mere idea had him grinning.

"What are you thinking?"

"That you have a beautiful smile."

"I'm not smiling," she unnecessarily pointed out, focusing on the auctioneer at the front of the crowded room.

"You should be. I like your smile. You should always smile, Joni."

"No one smiles all the time."

"But you usually do keep a smile on your face." She had one on her face this very second. "It's one of the many things I like about you."

She shifted in her chair. "You don't even know me, Grant. Not really."

"I've been trying to get to know you for weeks, but you keep shooting me down."

"I figured you'd lose interest."

"You aren't the kind of woman a man loses interest in, Joni. Not by a long shot."

Her eyes glazed over slightly, as if she was lost

in the past, making him wish he could read her mind, know what she was thinking. But shaking off whatever had momentarily clouded her mood, she grinned. "Well, even during the worst of times I've never been accused of being boring, that's for sure."

He'd like to have asked about her worst of times, but didn't want her mind going back to whatever she'd been thinking. Not when she was with him. When she was with him he wanted her to be all smiles. He wanted her to be all smiles all the time.

A hot-air balloon-ride package that a local company had donated came up for bid and an idea hit him. One involving him and Joni floating high in the sky, the feel of her lips much more thrilling than flying.

"You ever been up in a hot-air balloon?"

Surprise lighting her eyes, she shook her head. "No, I'd like to, but it isn't the kind of thing I'd do by myself."

Which was a telling statement. Just how long had she isolated herself? "Why not?"

A flash of confusion crossed her face, then she

shrugged. "You're right. It's on my bucket list, so why not? I can take my mom."

She raised her hand to bid, but Grant jerked her arm down and raised his. She attempted to pull his hand down as he'd done hers, but to no avail.

She tugged harder. "What are you doing?"

"Winning that package."

"Why? I was bidding."

The auctioneer rattled off more numbers, found another bidder, but Grant instantly countered.

"The package is for a romantic sunset flight for two. If I win, will you go with me, Joni? I'd say your mom could go with us, but the package is for two." He winked. "Too bad."

Not that he wouldn't like to meet Joni's mother. He would.

Joni didn't smile, but her lips twitched. "Is this your way of asking me out on a date again, Grant?"

"Depends. Is it working? Because so far the more traditional method hasn't proven effective."

"Okay," she agreed on a breathy sigh. "If you win the hot-air balloon package, I'll be your date, go up in the balloon with you and watch the sun go down in a blaze of colors, but only on one condition."

"What would that be?" Please don't say that your mother gets to go too. He'd probably be bad enough to need his hands slapped a few times, but he didn't want Mommy Dearest tagging along to chaperone.

"That you help me mark off another item on my bucket list."

"What would that be?"

Her eyes shone like magic, drawing him under her spell. "To be kissed in a hot-air balloon."

That was on her bucket list?

"Kiss you in a hot-air balloon?" The thought of her mouth pressed to his had him raising his hand higher when someone outbid him yet again. "It would be my pleasure."

Hand on his shoulder to steady herself, she stretched close and whispered into his ear, "Actually, I'm counting on it being my pleasure. You did promise you were really good."

Without hesitation, he stood, called out a bid that silenced the room and even left the auctioneer slack-jawed.

When he was announced the winner, Grant turned to Joni and grinned smugly. "If pleasure is your theme, you should add me to your bucket list."

CHAPTER FIVE

"LET me get this straight." Puckering her lips at herself in the bathroom mirror, Samantha rolled the tube of lip gloss down and slid on the cap. "You were on your way out of here with a man intent on ravaging you and you walked away when his boss stopped him to introduce his daughter?"

Yep, that about summed it up. Staring at her wild-eyed, rosy-cheeked reflection, Joni nodded. The night hadn't been dull, that was for sure.

Meeting her gaze in the mirror, Samantha shook her head in disbelief. "Honey, that's when you were supposed to put your hand around him to get the message across that he was your man."

Right. That was so her style. "But he's not my man."

"Duh." Samantha gave her that look that said

she wasn't having her brightest moment. "He won't ever be if you don't get your act together."

"I don't want him to be my man." Joni took the lipstick Samantha handed her and decided why not? She usually didn't wear anything more than balm or gloss, but the shade did look great on Samantha. Of course, everything looked great with Samantha's silky black hair and deep blue eyes. "Not really. I mean, I agreed to go on that hot-air balloon trip with him." And had made that quip about pleasure. "After all, he paid a small fortune for the bid, so how could I back out?"

Especially when his eyes had promised untold pleasures she ached to sample. Add him to her bucket list. Ha, he'd top the list. All other adventures would dull in comparison.

"You can't not go," Samantha agreed. "His bid was impressive, quite romantic."

"You might want romance, Samantha, but I don't." She wanted…what? Pleasure? She did want pleasure. Physical pleasure. But not romance. Romance created expectations that broke hearts. She didn't want a broken heart again.

Stretching her mouth open, she ran the lipstick over her lips, rubbed her lips together and inspected the effect. "I just want to use Grant for sex."

"Do what?"

Joni's hand jerked at Samantha's loud exclamation, smearing lipstick across the corner of her mouth and causing her to frown.

"You are going to have to repeat what you just said because I have lost my hearing. Or my mind. You totally did not just say what I think you just said."

Joni glanced toward the empty stalls to reassure herself there were no eavesdroppers, intentional or otherwise. She took a deep breath, then tried to explain her comment to her best friend. "I don't want a relationship with Grant or with any man. Relationships are messy and stress I don't need. But I am attracted to him. I just want to have sex with him. Really good, really hot, blow-my-mind sex."

Did that sound as horrible as she feared? She grimaced and waited for Samantha's verdict, knowing without doubt her friend wouldn't hold back. Samantha stared in wide-eyed silence.

"He probably wouldn't be okay with that, would he?" Joni's grimace deepened. "Should I just forget the whole thing? I should, shouldn't I?"

Samantha shook her head slowly. "He's a man. He'll be okay with you wanting to have sex with him. And, no, I don't think you need to forget the whole thing. Far from it."

Joni breathed a mental sigh of relief. If her best friend wasn't telling her she was a fool, then maybe she wasn't. Then again, men did it all the time. Why not her?

Samantha gave a concerned look. "What I need to know is whether or not you're really okay with that because I have trouble believing that you are."

"Of course I'm okay with it," Joni assured her friend. She wanted this. She wanted Grant. What she didn't want was to get hurt. "Relationships are complicated, especially between co-workers. I'm not willing to put my job in jeopardy." Been there, done that. "But if I go into this with my eyes wide open and abide by the rules, everything should be fine."

Looking skeptical, Samantha leaned against the bathroom sink. "Rules are meant to be broken."

Joni frowned. "No, they're not. Rules are meant to keep life orderly, to avoid problems by having a structured set of expectations. If I lay out the rules of our affair and Grant agrees to them, everything will be fine."

Samantha remained quiet a few seconds, then shrugged and smiled. "If it gets you to have a little fun, I say go for it."

Joni wasn't sure how to take Samantha's comment. She wanted her friend's approval, wanted her to think her plan brilliant. Instead, she sounded as if she thought Joni led a boring life. "Boredom has nothing to do with why I want Grant."

Samantha's brow quirked at her claim. "I'm sure it doesn't, but that doesn't mean you aren't ready for a little adventure in your life."

"I do have fun," Joni insisted with perhaps a little too much force. She enjoyed her life. Her calm, stable life that Grant had thrown such a wrench into. But Samantha had a point. Something had been missing. Maybe she hadn't acknowledged it even to herself, but she had begun to experience restlessness even before Grant had arrived on the scene. "But not as much fun as I'm going to have for however long this chemistry thing lasts between Grant and I."

"That's my girl."

Joni gestured to the make-up pouch Samantha was dropping back into her oversized purse. "Do you have something you can do my eyes with? I want to knock that man's socks off."

Samantha handed her the make-up. "Honey, it's not his socks you want to knock off. Let's aim for another, better piece of clothing." Samantha waggled her brows. "Like his boxers."

Grant finished paying for the bid he'd won and collected the raffle basket Joni had won while she'd been in the bathroom. She and Samantha had been gone long enough that Grant was beginning to wonder if Joni had flown the coop. He wouldn't be surprised. Not after the disappearing act she'd pulled while he'd been talking to Dr. Abellano.

He and Vann stood in silence in the hallway along with dozens of others. They'd been making idle chit-chat but Grant sensed the other man's unease at how long the women had been gone, too.

So when Heather came up to him and began asking questions about the ICU and his practice, Grant welcomed the distraction.

Vann's gaze lit on someone down the hallway and the man sighed with relief. Grant turned to greet the women, but stopped short when he saw Joni. She was always beautiful, but there was something different about her as she made her way toward him. Her gaze locked on his, she didn't look away, just came closer. Make-up, he realized. Joni had put on make-up. Not a lot, but enough to accent her pretty eyes and draw attention to her high cheekbones and plump lips.

Wow. She really was beautiful.

Her big green eyes never wavered as she walked right up to him, so close he could smell the sweet jasmine scent of her. The scent that had forever imprinted into his mind on the day he'd kissed her in the elevator.

Ignoring the others, she touched his shoulder and stretched on tiptoe, leaned close to his ear. "Let's go."

Grant didn't have to be told twice. Balancing the raffle basket on one hip, he absently nodded goodbye to the others, took Joni's hand, and made a bee-line for the closest exit.

"Is your car here?" he asked when they reached the still more than half-full parking lot.

She nodded, pointing out her little silver sedan. "Follow me to my place?"

"Lady, I'd follow you to hell and back."

Glancing up at him from behind thick eye-lashes, she smiled with feminine power. "No trip to hell required, although I don't doubt you've been there a time or two. But things may get that hot before the night is over."

"I hope so." He groaned, put the basket into the back seat of her car, then pulled her to him and studied her pretty upturned face. What had transpired in the bathroom? "I want you, Joni, but if you're not sure…"

"I'm sure." She kissed him to prove her point, but rather than deepen the kiss she jumped into the driver seat of her car, spouted off her address in case he got separated, and gave a little wave. "Keep up if you can."

Grant stood there a moment, blown away by the woman backing out of her parking spot. After weeks of running, Joni had finally realized they could be good together, that a relationship between them could work.

Good, he wanted a relationship with her. He wanted a lot of things with her, getting hot topping the list.

They sizzled any time they were near each other. He couldn't wait to get her out of those clothes, to kiss her, to taste the moist sweetness of her body and have her cry out his name with bliss, to have her throbbing with need, exploding with pleasure.

Grant raced to his car and started the engine.

His internal engine was already revved and raring to go.

Vroom. Vroom.

Grant pulled into Joni's driveway right behind

her, was out of his Hummer before she'd even killed her ignition.

Taking a deep breath, she reminded herself she was in control. This was what she wanted.

So why did she feel so awkward? Like what they were doing was so calculated?

Grant opened her door, extended his hand toward her.

She hesitated only a second before she put her hand in his, but her slight pause was enough to raise a red flag.

"Having second thoughts?" he asked as, hand in hand, they stepped onto her front porch.

Could the man read her mind or what?

"No," she assured him, sounding more confident than perhaps she was. Extracting her hand from his, she unlocked the house door and they stepped just inside the entranceway. "I want you."

"I want you, too. So much, Joni." He pulled her into his arms and kissed her lips, her throat, the hollow of her neck. "I think I've wanted you from the moment I first saw you."

A soft moan escaped her lips as she lost herself in the sweet sensations his every touch elicited.

The man's mouth was a phenomenon. So talented. So unreal. So intent on giving her promised pleasure.

His hands weren't anything to scoff at either. Oh, no. When he ran his palms over her arms, she shivered. When his fingers dug into her hair and pulled her closer, she quivered. When he slid his hand beneath her shirt, cupped her breast, tweaked his fingertip over her straining nipple, she almost melted into a puddle on the foyer floor.

"Take me to my bedroom," she ordered. Or had she been begging?

He grunted a response, but Joni couldn't make out his words. He scooped her into his arms and her belly fluttered with excitement. Had she died and gone to heaven? No, Grant hailed from the other direction. With as hot as his kiss burned, she was sure he did. Still…

"Which way?"

Her face pressed against the hard strength of his chest, she pointed towards her bedroom. She rubbed her cheek back and forth over his cotton-blend shirt, breathing in the wonderfully masculine smell of him. "It's the second door on the left."

She squinted when he turned on the overhead light, wanted him to turn it back off, but he refused.

"I want to see you, Joni," he said, stroking his hands over her. "I want to see every reaction to my touch. I want to see you respond."

She wanted to see him, too. Wanted to know if he was as buff as his body hinted at beneath his clothes. As rock solid as he felt against her body right at that very moment.

He whipped her black and white comforter and sheet back in one motion, placed her gently on her bed. Lying on her bed, she watched his every move, mesmerized. He kicked off his shoes. Grabbing the hem of his shirt, he lifted it over his head.

Joni's breath caught at the sight of his broad shoulders and chiseled abdomen. Oh, wow. The man should never wear a shirt. Not ever.

She reached for him, ran her hands over the cut planes, then rose up enough to place a kiss just above his navel.

The muscles beneath her lips tightened. He sucked in a deep breath. The sheer wonder that this beautiful man wanted her, that he was there with her, planned to make love to her, was so affected by her touch, blew her mind.

She needed to tell him her rules, to make sure he was okay to abide by them. But his fingers were in her hair and her mouth was too busy exploring his belly to actually form words.

She liked the growling noise he made when she accidentally brushed against the crotch of his jeans. She liked it so much that she stroked her fingers there again, purposefully, while she traced her tongue beneath his navel to tease just above his waistband.

"Joni," he groaned, his fingers twisting in her hair, not painfully but almost. Realizing what he was doing, he let go, slid his fingers free from her locks. "Stop."

Her heart fell. Had she done something wrong? Or had he changed his mind? Biting the raw inside of her lower lip, she lifted her head to look at him just as she closed her fingers over his zipper. Didn't he know she didn't want to stop? She wanted to touch him, to taste him, to be the one to give him pleasure, to be the one to whom he gave pleasure.

"You want me to stop?" Did she sound as disappointed as she felt?

"You have me on edge." His voice sounded strained, as if he really was on a high cliff and was about to topple off.

Understanding dawning, she stared at him, stunned. "But we've barely started."

"I know," he said with more than a tad of frustration. "But I've wanted you so long it's not going to take much. I want to be good for you, to give you every iota of pleasure I promised. At the rate we're going it's going to be over before we get started."

Wow. Knowing he was so turned on—by her!—was making this better and better, made her insides melt with definite pleasure.

Slowly and with a determined smile, she lowered his zipper, slid her fingers inside his jeans and tugged the material downwards.

* * *

With a groan Grant let Joni strip him, let her take in the sight of his naked body. Damn, he wanted her. Wanted to rip off her clothes and plunge inside her body until they both cried out in ecstasy. He wanted more from Joni than sex. He would force his body under enough control to take his time, to have her on edge as much as he was, to make sure she toppled into orgasmic bliss over and over before he lost his control.

Part of him questioned if they weren't rushing things. But he couldn't stop her, couldn't stop himself.

"You are way overdressed." Something he set about remedying. She reached to pull off her clothes, but Grant placed his hands over hers, staying her. He wanted to do this, to take her clothes off this first time, to enjoy each new inch of her exposed body. This was one journey he wanted to take slowly, to stop, smell the jasmine, and not miss one thing.

He pushed the material of her sweater upwards, exposing the milky flesh of her belly and placing a lingering kiss to her navel. How many times had he fantasized about taking off her sweater?

Just the reality that he was actually doing so was enough to make him throb.

His tongue danced in and out of her navel in slow, tantalizing strokes. He cupped her hips, slid his palms around to cup her round bottom, arching her off the bed, trying to pull her closer and closer, his mouth supping on her while he finished undressing her. When he finally removed the last of her clothes and she lay naked beneath him, he rose to take in her loveliness.

Softly moaning, she reached to pull him back, her greedy hands tugging him toward her. Still, he was in no rush, just soaked in the sight of Joni unleashed.

Her curvy little body stretched out on the sheets beckoned for him to run his fingers over every inch of her, to taste every inch of her, burn everything about her into his memory for all time.

"You are beautiful." He barely recognized his voice, could barely vocalize. Yet her beauty deserved poetic words his tongue could never do justice to. She deserved everything he could give and more.

"Thank you." Her cheeks bloomed rosily, her

lashes lowering a brief moment before lifting to reveal her desire-filled green eyes. "You're beautiful, too."

Him beautiful? It was enough to make him laugh, but her fingers had begun exploring his body again and the noise that came from his throat sounded more a growl. Touch after touch, kiss after kiss, they explored each other, stroking each other higher and higher until she whimpered with need and he couldn't hold back any longer.

He had to be inside her.

Donning a condom from his wallet, he moved over her. As he spread her creamy thighs, the only sound he could make was a grunt of acknowledgement. No poetry there.

But nothing had ever been written that compared to the desire he saw in Joni's eyes when he pushed into the moist softness of her body, to the gut-wrenching pleasure that shook his body with each thrust inside. Deeper and deeper.

Her fingers dug into his buttocks, gripping him tight, urging him faster, harder, pushing him over that edge he was dangling so close to, that edge he didn't want to fall over quite yet, but couldn't fight any longer.

"Grant," she cried, her body spasming around him, contracting tighter and tighter. "I need you now!"

"Joni," he growled between gritted teeth, giving in to the urgency in his groin, giving in to the feminine call of her body. He spilt himself deep inside her and toppled over into satisfaction he'd never known.

CHAPTER SIX

DESPITE having her face practically buried in her pillow, Joni winced at the sunlight peeking in around the shades that mostly blocked the brightness from her bedroom.

Morning already?

Urgh. Why did she feel like a truck had run over her?

Because a Grant truck had run over her.

And into her.

What had she done?

Not rising from where she lay on her belly, she prised one eye open slightly, letting her surroundings come into focus. Over the edge of her pillow she saw evidence of exactly what she'd done.

More like whom she'd done.

Sleeping on his belly, too, Grant lay sprawled on her full-sized bed, taking up more than his fair share of mattress real estate. Thank God he was still asleep so she could escape and…and, well, she wasn't quite sure what she was going to do at this point. She'd never had a morning after. Mark had always gone home not long after finishing his business—which had never taken long. Until last night she hadn't had anything to compare Mark's quickies to. Now that she did, well, quickie was the only description that fit.

Grant hadn't been quick. Oh, no. The man had taken his time and taken her to a whole new plateau of sensations. She was pretty sure that last night in his arms she'd developed a sixth sense. A sexual sense.

Or maybe just a Grant sense.

He'd touched every part of her body, tasted every part of her body, had continued to touch her even afterwards, almost as if he hadn't been able not to.

Memories of all he had done filling her mind, she studied him. His dark lashes fanned over his strong cheek bones. Beautiful and tousled and way too sexy in sleep.

Asleep or awake didn't matter. The man was way too sexy, period.

For some crazy reason he'd found her sexy, too, had told her over and over during the night how much he wanted her, how crazy she drove him, how he'd been fighting the urge to touch her since they'd first met. Even now, he had one hand possessively cupping her bottom.

How many times during the night had he told her how much he liked her bottom? That when he looked at her round curves it was all he could do to keep from pushing her legs apart and thrusting deep inside her body?

Not that he hadn't done that. Multiple times.

He had. Yet each time they'd had sex hadn't been any less urgent, any less heated when they'd come together.

How many times during the long night had they…three…four? Not a quickie amongst them. A smile spread across her face. No wonder she felt like she'd had a head-on collision with an eighteen-wheeler.

Doing her best not to wake him, she wiggled free of his hand, rolled onto her side, and stared at the man who'd done such amazing things to her body throughout the night.

They hadn't been awkward. Had someone asked her if they would have been, she'd have argued they would. Even months into their relationship she'd still felt awkward with Mark, had preferred the lights off when they'd had sex. He hadn't minded, had told her on more than one occasion she should diet.

Grant had minded. Had insisted the lights be on that first time, had taken in every aspect of her nakedness with eager eyes. So how could she possibly not have felt awkward when she'd been so thoroughly inspected by a man as beautiful as Grant with the lights on?

Yet he'd looked at her with such desire, touched her with such reverence and need of his own, that awkwardness just hadn't been an issue. He'd made her feel beautiful, desirable, as if she were the sexiest woman alive.

Or maybe she'd been so consumed with desire that her own need had waylaid any awkwardness that might have arisen.

Regardless, she'd felt divine in his arms. Decadent and desirable and sexy.

Her gaze slid over the defined contours of his body, over the muscles of his back, the dip of his spine just at where her sheet bunched low on his hips, revealing just a glimpse of his tight buttocks.

She'd known he had a great behind.

He had a great everything. From the chiseled planes of his chest and abdomen to the sinewy lines of his thighs to the strong arms that had held her all night. His body was perfect. He was perfect.

He'd been generous, tender, demanding, giving, and had made her feel like the most desirable woman in the world. When he'd looked at her, she'd felt like the only woman in the world. As if he really cared about her.

Which was insane.

She didn't need to go repeating history. She'd made the mistake once of reading more into sex than just sex. Not that sex with Mark had come close to what she'd experienced at the mercy of Grant's talented body.

Try as she might, she couldn't even picture Mark's body, even his face seemed fuzzy in her mind. Odd as once upon a time the man had occupied all her thoughts, had been the center of her world.

Had almost cost her everything. Had he really thought she'd turn her back on her mother? Even if he hadn't cheated on her, she would have stood by her mother always. To add insult to injury, he'd used his professional role at the hospital to raise doubts about her nursing abilities after he'd already tattered her heart with his cheating ways.

No, she wouldn't be making the same mistakes again.

This time she was going to be the one to call the shots, to make the rules.

Perhaps she should have laid them out to Grant before they'd spent the night tangled in her sheets, but better late than never.

Better now than later.

"Wake up." She shook his shoulder. "We need to talk."

One sleepy blue eye popped open, then the other. A lazy, self-satisfied grin slid onto his handsome face. Joni's heart skipped a beat, begging her to forget talking and jump the man's bones instead. Really, how often did she wake up with a gorgeous, smiling hunk in her bed? Never.

"Morning, darling."

Her insides melted to a warm, gushy ooze. A gorgeous, smiling hunk in her bed who called her darling! Pathetic! She was easy if that was all it took to get her juices flowing.

The man had only to exist to make her juices flow.

"We need to talk," she repeated, determined not to be distracted by the warm, gushy oozy flow.

He rolled onto his side, yawned, stretching out his arm high above his body, emphasizing each and every muscle along his ripped ribs and belly.

Oh, me, oh, my! Joni's insides caught fire.

"This the part where you tell me this was a mistake and kick me out?" He looked more amused than worried.

Hardly. "This probably was a mistake and I should kick you out but, no, that's not what we need to talk about."

He gave a mock sigh of relief. "Good, because

I'm hungry. Whatcha got that I can rustle us up for breakfast? We can talk while we eat."

Keeping the sheet pulled up over her naked breasts—why hadn't she put on clothes before waking him?—she shook her head. "Breakfast isn't what I want."

His brow lifted. But rather than take her seriously, his eyes twinkled with mischief. "You hungry for something else?"

"Not that either," she quickly assured him, tightening her grip on the sheet. She did want that, had wanted that from the moment she'd awakened and realized he was still in bed with her. Crazy. "Now," she scolded, determined to see this through, "be serious. I need to lay down the ground rules."

"You're what I'd like to lay down." He waggled his brows at her, scooted up on his pillow. "What ground rules?"

Ignoring how the sheet dipped seriously low over his waist, revealing a happy trail she'd like to walk down, she toughened her resolve. "My ground rules for what happened last night."

She didn't have to tell him to be serious now. His expression grew guarded. "Which are?"

"That this means nothing."

He had the audacity to laugh. "Lady, if you believe that, you're crazy."

She didn't like it that he was laughing at her. "Last night was amazing, but we both know it didn't mean anything." When he started to interrupt, she held up her hand. "It didn't. Not beyond phenomenal sex."

"It meant something to me."

Her heart skipped a beat. Or ten.

"I'm not interested in a serious relationship," she warned, not wanting him to say things he didn't mean just because they were in bed. She'd heard men said what they thought women wanted to hear. Mark certainly had. He'd said all the right things and not meant one. She didn't want false platitudes.

"I'm not interested in casual sex," he countered, so smoothly she could almost believe him. Almost.

"We haven't been out on a single date, haven't had any kind of relationship outside the hospital.

How could last night be anything other than casual sex?" See, she could be logical. She sounded logical. Only the wild beating of her heart hinted that more than logic might be at play.

"Only because you refused to go out with me when I asked you out," he reminded her, then sighed. "You're right. We probably should have waited, but last night was a lot more than casual sex. There's powerful chemistry between us."

He shifted toward her, exposing a glimpse of what treasure lay at the end of his particular happy trail. La la la, she so wasn't going to stare...even if she wanted to.

Oh, yeah. Logic. She was supposed to be logical. "Chemistry is just lust, Grant."

Just as her reactions to him were just lust. Nothing more.

He didn't bother pulling up the sheet to cover what he'd partially exposed, just shrugged. "If you say so."

"I say so."

His expression unreadable, he studied her for a few moments, then grinned that half-cocked grin that hinted he knew a lot more than she gave him credit for. "That your only 'rule'? That last night be defined as just chemistry?"

This time she laughed, but partially to hide her discomfort at their conversation. "Hardly."

"You gonna tell me the rest of your rules, Lil Miss Control Freak?" He didn't appear in the slightest nonplussed, just amused, as if she was a child he was humoring.

"Don't mock me, Grant."

"I wouldn't dare." He grinned, doing just that. "You have the good stuff, and I want more." His gaze skimmed over her face, her throat, her shoulders. "Lots more. Tell me what I've got to do to get more."

Joni gulped. Why hadn't she gotten dressed, brushed her teeth, combed her hair, and put on some lip gloss? Anything to help improve her look first thing in the morning.

Then again, Grant didn't seem to mind in the slightest the way she looked all tousled and wild haired. Actually, if what was peeking out from beneath the sheet was anything to go on, he really liked how she looked. A lot.

"I do," he said, almost with a growl.

Startled, her gaze shot to his. "You do what?"

"Want you."

"I didn't say you wanted me."

"You didn't have to." He brushed a hair away from her temple, cupped her face. "Now, tell me about these rules I have to abide by so I can make love to you."

How was she supposed to tell him her rules when he looked at her like that? When she could see on his face that he was remembering what they'd done throughout the night and he wanted to do all that again? When she wanted him to do all that again?

"I don't want anyone to know," she rushed out.

His fingers stilled. "Huh?"

"I don't want anyone to know we're having an affair. That way when we end there won't be any fuss and muss at work." They'd just stop having sex and that would be the end of it. No worries about any negative impact on her career. No looks of sympathy from her co-workers. Nothing. Just a clean break.

His brow quirked. "Do you really think that's possible after last night?"

Her face burned. "No one knows about last night."

He didn't look convinced. "You think no one saw us leave together?"

He made a good point, but they had taken different vehicles. "That doesn't mean they know you came here or that they know what we did."

"Anyone who saw me look at you knows exactly what we did last night. I wanted you, Joni." He stroked his thumb across her cheek. "I still do."

She wanted him, too, but she was not going to get distracted from her rules. Not again. Because she really should have laid them out prior to them having sex and the longer she delayed the harder it would be to play by them. She needed those rules. Without them she was nothing more than a sitting duck waiting to have her heart trampled on.

"No touching me at work," she said.

"But touching you in private is okay?" His fingers brushed down her throat, touching her in private quite nicely.

"Private is okay." More than okay. "In private, I want you to touch me."

"Good, because I like touching you." His finger traced over her collarbone, over her chest to toy at where she clutched the sheet to her breasts. "I like touching you a lot."

She liked him touching her a lot, too. Wowzers, but the man had magic hands.

"Don't ask me personal things." Never would a man use her mother's alcoholism against her again. Even though her mother had been dry for almost five years, had recently married and was happier than she'd ever been, Joni wouldn't let a man close enough to throw rocks at the fragile glass house protecting her mother.

"As in?"

"Like about my family and past, that kind of thing."

His lips twisted and for a moment she thought he was going to balk, but instead his finger began dancing over her again.

"Any more rules?" he asked, dipping to blow warm breath against the curve of her neck.

Shivers ran up and down her spine.

She took a deep breath and spat out the one that had hurt her most. False words of love. Words she'd heard once but that had been fabrication. Never did she want to hear such lies again. Never. "Don't tell me you love me."

Grant straightened, his hand falling away from her body. "Pardon?"

"Don't say I love you or things like that. I don't want to hear mushy pleasantries or have you do mushy things like flowers or candy that make implications that this is a relationship leading anywhere other than mutual physical satisfaction."

Not that she thought he would do any of those things, but if she'd laid down the law that he couldn't, then she'd never be disappointed when he didn't.

Grant shook his head as if to clear his thoughts. "Let me get this straight. We're going to have an affair, not let anyone know. I'm not to ask anything personal and can't tell you I love you or do 'mushy' things for you, and I can only touch you in private?"

She nodded.

His brow quirked high. "That it?"

"For now."

His gaze narrowed. "You get to make up new rules as we go?"

She hadn't thought that far ahead, but it sounded good to her. "Is that a problem?"

"Possibly." He shrugged. "Depends on the rule."

"If you don't like the rule, you don't have to play." Did she sound as much like a petulant child as she felt?

He regarded her long moments. "If I opted not to play?"

Her heart squeezed tightly in her chest, but she kept her expression bland. She waved her fingers in a bye-bye motion.

"So, it's your way or the highway?" He made it sound so crass, so unyielding, but he didn't look miffed, just amused as always.

Which annoyed her. And worried her. But she wasn't going to back down. She couldn't. She needed those rules for her own survival. Without them she might fall in love with Grant, might end up with a broken heart again, might end up having to fight to keep her job again.

"Those are my rules for now. Take them or leave them."

Why was she holding her breath? Why did her every cell seem to be anxiously awaiting his response? What if he said no? Then what? Could she really say goodbye after what they'd shared during the night? Could she really deny herself that pleasure, deny herself him?

"Oh, I'm going to take 'em," he assured her, running his finger through his hair. "No doubt about it. I just want to make sure I understand your terms so there's no confusion down the road."

"I will clarify anything you aren't sure about."

"We are having a sex-only relationship?"

Joni thought about it. Pretty much that was what she'd outlined. Their lives would be less entangled when they broke up. Eventually, they would. If he only encompassed one part of her life, moving on would be so much easier. She wouldn't be as devastated as she'd been with Mark's multiple betrayal. Sex-only was a good plan.

"Sex is all I want from you." Why did she feel a bit nauseated at her words? She wasn't a sex-only kind of woman. Well, she hadn't been a sex at all kind of woman for the past five years. After last night she'd realized what she'd been missing out on all these years. She didn't want to go back to celibacy. No way. "I want sex from you, Grant."

He regarded her as if he couldn't quite believe what he was hearing. "At work we pretend we're, what? Just friends? Nothing at all?"

"Nothing about our relationship at work needs to change. We will go on as we have always gone on. Professionally, but nothing more."

"You really think that's possible?"

Of course. Otherwise he shouldn't be in her bed.

"Why wouldn't it be?"

"Because every time I look at you I'm going to want to touch you."

"You're not allowed to touch me except in private."

"And in my mind," he added. "When I see you

at the hospital, I'm going to remember what you look like without those scrubs on and in my mind I'm going to touch."

She would probably be doing some mental touching of her own, but she wasn't going to tell him that.

"I'm allowed to touch you in private?" His expression took on a wicked gleam. Or maybe it was that he was smiling that smile that said he knew her thoughts and liked them. "If we end up alone in a supply closet, I have to keep my hands to myself?"

The man was too much.

"If we end up alone in a supply closet, it'll be because you've pulled me into that supply closet."

His gaze traced over her face, lower. "You think?"

He wasn't even touching her. Why was her skin tingling? Why were her thighs clenching? She held the sheet tighter to her, kept her arms over her breasts.

"I don't go hanging out in hospital supply closets of my own accord." But if doing so meant he would touch her, she just might set up camp. She wanted him touching her. Right now, she wanted him touching her.

He might not physically be touching her, but his gaze was blazing a hot trail down her throat, making her imagine his hands there, making her imagine his mouth there.

His brow arched. "But you might develop the habit?"

This was so unfair. The man was turning her on without laying a finger on her. How did that work? She started to bite her lip, realized what she was doing and wet them instead. "Hasn't been a problem in the past."

"A shame. You've really been missing out." His eyes met hers, held, mesmerized. "Maybe you should try it some time."

She swallowed. "Me? Or we?"

"Well, if you're offering…"

"That would break my own rule before we even got started."

His gaze bored into hers, deep and intense and for once more serious than amused. "Rules are meant to be broken, Joni."

Wasn't that exactly what Samantha had warned?

"No," she quickly denied, not liking his suddenly solemn expression. Although perhaps she should. That meant he was taking her rules under sincere consideration, right? "My rules are to protect us. Both of us."

"I don't need protecting, Joni. Not from you."

"Sure you do." Her tone was light, teasing. Why, she didn't know, because she wanted to be taken seriously, but she wanted his smile back on his face, wanted the intense expression he wore gone. "You don't even know me. Not my likes or dislikes. Not my bad habits. Not my pet peeves. Nothing. Not to mention I'm a crazy mixed-up woman who is laying down rules for our relationship."

"I know enough and the rest I'll learn," he said, scooting further back against the bed's headboard. "At least you're being upfront about where you stand and what you want from me. That's more than most women do."

Had he been hurt in the past? Had some woman not been upfront? Just the thought caused a pinch in her chest that she barely acknowledged, much less attempted to label.

She picked up a pillow, straightened the cotton case around the spongy material, attempting to smooth the wrinkles. "I don't want either of us to get hurt. Rules are to keep people safe."

Grant's hand covered hers, smoothing her palm over the cool cotton. "Everyone gets hurt, Joni." He flipped her hand to lace her fingers with his. "One just has to decide who is worth getting hurt for and who isn't."

His hand felt so good holding hers, so right. Yet his words…

"That's a pessimistic attitude," she accused, wanting to diffuse the conversation, to move to something lighter, more fun.

Taking her cue, he laughed. "This coming from the woman who just laid down rules to clearly draw the lines of our relationship as purely physical because she's afraid to have a real relationship because one of us might get hurt."

He gave a mock sigh and shook his gorgeous head.

"Not wanting a real relationship with you and being afraid to have one are two very different things," she pointed out, wanting to be sure he understood, wanting to be sure she understood. She wasn't afraid. She just didn't want the messy fall-out that would come when they ended. She didn't fool herself that they wouldn't end. She knew they would. Planning ahead was not the same thing as fear.

"You're not afraid of us?"

"No," she denied. Fear had nothing to do with her rules. Prevention was just good medicine. As a doctor, he should know that. Having rules in place to keep either of them from having unrealistic expectations was just smart.

"I am," he surprised her by admitting, lifting her hand to his lips to place a soft kiss against her knuckles. "I'm terrified that I'm in bed with a control freak who wants to talk about rules and relationship boundaries when we are alone and naked and should be giving each other a great deal of pleasure. Scary stuff."

His lips lingered against her hand, rubbing gently back and forth. His caress caused thunder to roar inside her body. Her heart beat wildly in her chest. Her lungs flopped around, forgetting to take in vital oxygen. Her blood quivered through her veins, anticipating what he'd do next.

"That scares you?" she whispered, watching him closely, thinking him the most beautiful man she'd ever seen. Maybe not physically, although perhaps, but there was something about him, something that made him stand out above the crowd.

Then he smiled and her every body function stalled.

Mrs. Sain was right. It was his smile.

The smile that was just for her, Joni. That beautiful smile that made you feel as if you were the center of his universe. That wicked smile that let you know he was thinking something naughty and you were the star of those naughty thoughts. The smile that said he enjoyed life and that for however long he graced you with his presence, you'd enjoy life too.

"Oh, yeah," he said softly. "That scares me."

The tip of his tongue poked into the sensitive skin between her fingers, rubbing in an erotic little motion that had her aching body surging to life, had her other hand twisting the sheet against her breasts.

"What are you going to do to make me not afraid any more?"

His tone was so seductive, so alluring, so full of the promise of pleasure, but she wasn't ready to acquiesce to him. She was the one in control here. He would do well to remember that.

"Turn on the lights?" she suggested, biting back a moan when his teeth nipped at her finger. Oh, heaven, that felt so good.

He shook his head. "Not going to work. It's not dark."

Telling herself not to give in to the pleasure his magical mouth was eliciting, not yet, she let her gaze follow that happy trail. "Tell you what a big gun you have?"

He paused, grinned. "That might distract me for a while."

"But wouldn't make you any less terrified?"

"Nope." He turned her hand palm up and she prepared for an onslaught of sensation as his tongue toyed with her palm. So when his lips supped against the delicate flesh of her wrist instead, sucking gently, she almost came.

"Maybe you should try again." He lifted his head to stare into her eyes. "Come up with something more creative to allay my fears."

He wanted her to try again? He wanted creative? She'd give him creative.

She let go of the sheet, letting the material drop to her waist and expose her bare chest. His audible sucking in of breath sent a surge of power through her, sent a thrill of pleasure ricocheting through her body. He wanted her. This man looked at her, even in the early morning when she needed a shower and toothbrush, and he wanted her so completely that the sight of her naked body had him catching his breath. Wow.

"Maybe..." she leaned forward, traced her fingertip along the downward path marking his flat belly, liking how his muscles contracted with her touch, liking how his eyes never left hers "...we shouldn't be talking at all."

CHAPTER SEVEN

"AS LONG as you behave, Dr. Bradley plans to transfer you to the regular medical floor today." Joni checked Mrs. Sain's telemetry, happy to see her vitals remained stable.

"Me behave?" The woman cackled with delight. "Since when have I ever behaved?"

"Not since I've known you, that's for sure," Joni agreed, winking at the smiling woman. "But I figure you're probably getting tired of hanging out around this place."

"This place isn't so bad. Around here I have hunky men coming into my room several times a day."

Uh-oh. "Hunky men?"

"Dr. Bradley."

"Ah." She so wasn't going there. Not with Mrs. Sain. Not with anyone. Samantha had already cornered her several times, trying to get her to spill the goods. Not happening. Mostly because what she and Grant shared had been private. Not something she wanted to impart. Not even to her best friend. For now what was between them was her happy little secret.

"You put that man out of his misery yet?"

Joni's gaze shot to her patient's. "What?"

"You know what." Mrs. Sain shook a bony, clubbed finger at her. "I may be old, but I'm not blind."

"That's questionable." Joni attempted to smother a smile and failed horribly. Seriously, how was she supposed to smother a smile when she felt so amazingly happy?

The woman cackled again. "You're going to give that boy a run for his money, aren't you?"

"I'm not going to give that boy—" which seemed like such a wrong descriptive label for Grant when he was definitely all man "—anything."

"That's a pity." Mrs. Sain shook her head as if sorely disappointed. "If I was fifty years younger, I'd give him anything he wanted and then some."

Joni bit back another smile. Yeah, she'd given Grant everything he wanted and then some, too. Or maybe it had been the other way around. He'd given her everything she wanted, amazing sex, agreed to her rules, left with no fuss, and hadn't bothered her since except to send her a few very suggestive text messages that had made her burst out laughing then sigh in giddy remembered pleasure.

Her mother had asked about the texts, but Joni hadn't even told her about Grant. He was her private secret. Sort of.

"No," she contradicted her patient, just to be as ornery as the older woman, mostly because Mrs. Sain liked the sparring. "You wouldn't. Fifty years ago you were happily married to Hickerson and wouldn't have even noticed another man."

"True." The woman nodded, closing her eyes for a moment and smiling at whatever memories floated through her mind. When she met Joni's gaze, she wore a happy expression even if her next words scolded. "But if you don't get busy, fifty years from now you aren't going to have memories to look back on."

Ha, what would Mrs. Sain say if she told her that she'd gotten busy Friday night with the very hunky Dr. Bradley? Very busy. Saturday morning, too, right up until they'd realized they hadn't had any more condoms. They'd improvised and Joni had no complaints about how satisfied he'd left her. No complaints whatsoever. The man could do amazing things with his mouth.

O-mazing things. And his little finger. And his big toe. And everything in between. Oh, yes, he could do O-mazing things.

"That's an odd smile on your face."

Joni didn't meet the woman's eyes, neither did she bother trying to hide the smile on her face. She couldn't have even if she had tried. What could she say? The man made her smile. He made her smile real big in a goofy kind of way.

"Well, you sly little girl." Mrs. Sain sounded pleased, as if she'd played matchmaker and was proud of her meddling ways. "It's about time."

"About time for what?" Grant stepped into the room, pulling his stethoscope from around his neck and flashing a smile at both ladies.

Joni immediately looked away, pretending to

be busy. She couldn't look at him. If she did she'd only confirm all the things Mrs. Sain thought she knew.

Unfortunately, she couldn't not look at him either.

How could she not look at him when just hearing his voice sent a jolt of joy through her veins?

She'd not seen him since he'd left her place Saturday afternoon. Not talked to him because she'd told him not to call. AA had taken up most of the day and night but Grant had never been far from her mind. Of course, his silly text messages had made sure he was never far from her mind. Good thing he'd reminded her after the first one that she'd said for him not to call, but hadn't mentioned a thing about texting.

When she'd crawled into bed she'd considered calling him, asking him over, but she figured she shouldn't get used to him in her bed every night. Plus, what if he'd changed his mind? What if once he was away from her he'd realized he didn't have to play by her rules? That there were hundreds of women who'd love to let him set the rules?

But if he'd decided any of those things, he wouldn't have texted her just before midnight to wish her sweet dreams, would he?

Obviously, he'd thought about her as much as she had him, had enjoyed their night together as much as she had. Just the thought made her want to dance around the ICU room.

"Her vitals are stable, Dr. Bradley." But mine aren't. Mine are going nuts because you're in the same room with me and all I can think is how much I'd like to strip those hospital scrubs off you and lick those fantastic abs.

"Thanks." He didn't look up at her, almost appeared to be purposely ignoring her. Then again, maybe he was.

Wow, they sounded out of place, stiff and too formal. Although she understood exactly why he wasn't teasing her as he usually did, she admitted that she missed the attention he usually showered on her.

Insane. He was giving her what she wanted. Sort of.

Mrs. Sain glanced back and forth between them, shaking her head. "Don't know what's wrong with young people these days. Back during my time we had common sense."

"We have common sense," Grant said, patting her hand.

The woman gave a perturbed shake of her head. "Not from where I'm lying."

"Which is what I'm here to discuss with you." Grant winked at his patient. "I'm transferring you to the medical floor this morning. If you remain stable there, I'll send you home in a few days."

"Home." The woman crinkled her already wrinkly nose. "Home is where the heart is. Can you send me there?"

Joni couldn't pull her gaze away from Grant. He still hadn't looked directly at her, just that flash of a smile when he'd come into the room, and then he'd poured all his attention on their patient. But something wistful played on his face, made Joni want to ask about his home, to know everything about him.

"Where would that be?" he asked their patient.

"Not at that assisted living facility, that's for sure. That place is more a prison than a home."

"We've discussed this. Your family moved you

there because they believe that's what's best for you. They didn't want you living alone anymore because it just wasn't a safe option."

"I know," she admitted on a resigned sigh. "I agree that they did what they believe is the right thing. I know I'm not a spring chicken anymore and need a little help from time to time and that's why they encouraged me to go there. It's also why I agreed because I didn't want them to feel guilty, because they shouldn't. I'm old and have lived my life. They need to get on with theirs." She stopped, took several deep inhalations through her nasal cannula, letting her oxygen saturation rise where it had fallen from her talking. "But," she continued, "that doesn't mean I have to like it. And that sure ain't where my heart is."

Joni listened to them chat while she entered data into the electronic medical record. Surreptiously, she studied Grant.

He looked great in his navy scrubs, especially now that she knew what those loose scrubs hid. The man had a gorgeous body.

And a killer smile that he was flashing Mrs. Sain's way.

Joni's heart flopped around like a fish out of water.

His mouth had kissed every inch of her, had made her back arch off her bed and her body go into total meltdown. She'd run her fingers over every inch of him, knew what his skin tasted like, knew how it felt to have him stretching her body, knew how it felt to orgasm mindlessly in his arms.

She'd done all that without feeling in the slightest bit embarrassed.

Now fully dressed and in a professional setting, she felt awkward and unsure. What was she supposed to say to him? How was she supposed to act?

Because what she really wanted to do was wrap her arms around him and tell him how happy she was to see him, how much his text messages had meant yesterday.

She'd been the one to lay down the laws of their relationship, but spouting out those rules while lying naked in bed with him had been one thing. Not wanting to have him smile at her and publicly acknowledge that something spectacular had happened between them quite another.

In theory, they were good rules.

But life wasn't theory. Life was real, just as Grant was real. Even if she hated to admit it, she was disappointed that he was ignoring her.

What had she wanted? Him to bombard her with roses and promises of forever after a single night in bed together?

Hardly. She just needed to get her act together, to abide by her own rules. If she couldn't do that, then she couldn't see Grant at all.

"If there's nothing I can do for you, Dr. Bradley, I'm going to go check on another patient." Perhaps her voice inflected a little too much coolness, but she needed to escape, to get away from his over-abundance of pheromones before she gave in to his allure and did something crazy. Like tackle him and drag his sexy behind beneath Mrs. Sain's hospital bed.

"Oh, there's something you can do for me, Nurse Joni. A lot of somethings."

Joni's jaw dropped. Had he really just said what

she thought he'd said or had she imagined his words? His implications?

With a devilish grin, he continued, "You can call the medical floor to have them prepare a bed for Mrs. Sain so we can get her transferred."

Mrs. Sain muttered something about him being bad, but Joni couldn't be sure because of the roaring in her ears. Or maybe it was the sizzling heat pouring off her face.

Blast him! He'd done that on purpose.

"Yes, sir," she said with a straight face and a tone that would have fit in perfectly had she clicked her heels together and saluted him.

"And you can…" He gave a couple of other medical orders. The things he said could be twisted into double meanings, but she didn't let on that he'd said anything out of the ordinary.

"Yes, sir," she repeated when he'd finished. She didn't meet his eyes, just stared at his ear and tried not to think about the fact she'd had that earlobe between her teeth not so very long ago. "I'll get right on that."

"Thanks," Grant said, without glancing up from where he'd pulled Mrs. Sain's last portable chest X-ray so he could review the digital film displayed on the computer monitor.

Joni glanced toward her patient, who watched them both curiously but who had thankfully remained gracefully quiet. Good. The last thing she needed was Mrs. Sain to comment on how goofily she'd been smiling earlier, about how totally infatuated she was with a man whom she was only supposed to be having a short-term physical relationship with.

"I'll be back to check on you in a little while," she promised her grinning patient. "And to get you ready for your big move."

Having stared at the lateral image of Mrs. Sain's chest X-ray so long he had commited it to memory, from the corner of his eye Grant watched Joni leave the room. When he turned back towards his patient he found wise old eyes watching him.

"Don't suppose you'd tell me what happened between you two this weekend?"

"Nope."

"Didn't figure you would." Mrs. Sain laughed, then cleared her throat with a cough.

"But you asked all the same."

"I'm old. If I ask or say things I shouldn't, people just put it down to me being senile."

Shaking his head, Grant grinned. "Only a fool would take you for senile. Your mind is sharper than most."

"Too bad this broken-down body can't keep up with what's still in here." She tapped the side of her head. "Up here I don't feel any different than when I was in my twenties."

Grant nodded. He'd heard others say similar things. The mind remained young, but the body wouldn't co-operate. Mind over matter didn't always hold true. Although he certainly gave credit to Mrs. Sain repeatedly pulling back from death's door to the fact that her attitude was full of gumption.

"You finally convinced her to go out with you?"

Speaking of gumption. "There you go with those senile questions again. I may have to order a CT scan of your brain if you keep that up." He winked. "Besides, you know every woman is beating down my doorway to get me to take her out."

"Uh-huh." Mrs. Sain didn't look convinced. Or senile. "Except for the one you want, and she's running scared. Although maybe she forgot her tennis shoes this weekend because I don't think she was running."

"Good thing you're not senile."

Mrs. Sain rolled her eyes, then scooted up in her bed. "Stick to your guns and give her time."

"Time?"

"To get past whatever has her running. She likes you and that scares her. Can't say I blame her. You pack a potent punch."

Grant tried not to wince at an eighty-year-old telling him he packed a potent punch.

"She'll come round."

He marked that he'd reviewed the chest X-ray and closed the radiology program within the EMR system. "That's what I'm hoping for."

He really shouldn't admit that to his patient, was probably being all kinds of unprofessional in doing so. But maybe he needed to talk to someone. Mrs. Sain seemed liked the logical choice regardless of however an unlikely one.

This time it was her bony hand patting his. "I know you are, son. It shows every time you look at her."

Was he that obvious? And why did something in his chest constrict at Mrs. Sain's "son"? Why did her endearment make him long to see his own mother and have her comfort him? Christine would think him crazy if he called her up and told her he wanted a visit. After all, there wasn't a holiday in sight.

"Maybe you should do something nice for her," Mrs. Sain continued, oblivious to his mind's crazy rambling. "Send her flowers or a box of chocolates. Women like that kind of thing so long as you're sincere about your intentions."

"Oh, I'm sincere about my intentions all right." He couldn't help but grin and waggle his eyebrows in his best bad-boy imitation. "But I have strict orders not to."

Mrs. Sain frowned. "She on a diet?"

"You might say that." Did Joni diet? She certainly didn't need to. Her curves were perfect.

She had dug into her food at the fundraiser with gusto, but in reality she hadn't eaten much off her plate.

"Well, flowers don't have calories." Mrs. Sain's face crinkled with thought. "Unless she has allergies. She have allergies to flowers?"

"Apparently so." He had no idea. He needed to spend more time with Joni so he knew the answers to questions like these. He needed to spend time with her so they could get to know each other and see where the attraction between them led.

"Hmm." Mrs. Sain became thoughtful. "Maybe you should talk to her friends, find out what she likes, then do something for her that would have special meaning. Women like it when you take the time to make the things you do for them personal."

"Not a senile bone in your body," he teased. "Don't let anyone tell you otherwise." He leaned down and gave the woman a peck on her forehead. "But I think I should stick with your first advice and give Joni time to figure out what she wants."

"It's a plan." Mrs. Sain's expression didn't convey that she thought it was a good plan, just a plan. "Just don't give her too much time or she'll think you aren't interested."

"I'm interested."

"I know." Mrs. Sain's eyes lit with excitement at his admission. "I just wondered if you knew. If she knew. Oh! I do know." She practically sat up in her hospital bed. "You could be a secret admirer. Soften her up by wooing her incognito."

"Wooing her incognito is about the only way she'll let me woo her." He laughed, letting the idea stir. He did want to woo Joni. He wanted to take her into his arms and tell her how amazing Friday night and Saturday morning had been, how he'd picked up his phone a hundred times the day before, wanting to call her, to hear her voice, to beg for an invitation back into her bed, even if just to hold her. Then again, according to Joni, the only invitations into her bed that she'd be issuing wouldn't be for sleeping or cuddling. She wanted action and nothing else. How ironic.

But wooing her incognito? Maybe. Definitely there would be a perverse satisfaction in rebelling against her ridiculous rules, and, really, could she blame him if she had a secret admirer?

"How'd you get so smart?" he asked the woman who watched him intently and had obviously read his every thought as it flitted across his face.

"You live long enough you learn a thing or two."

"I'll keep that in mind."

"You do that, and I'll keep thinking on a way to help you win her affections."

He didn't ask why his patient would be willing to do that. He figured lying in a hospital bed day and night she probably didn't have a lot of other things to focus on.

Besides, where Joni was concerned, he needed all the help he could get.

CHAPTER EIGHT

TRUE to his word, Grant ignored Joni at the hospital.

At least before, he'd always had a smile for her, always found a reason to accidentally touch her, talk to her.

Now nothing.

Not even a meeting of the eyes.

Four days had passed. Mrs. Sain had been transferred to another unit and Joni heard she'd been discharged from the hospital altogether that morning. She'd meant to say goodbye to the woman, but they'd had a code on the ICU floor and all chaos had broken loose. By the time she'd been able to take a break, Mrs. Sain had already left the hospital with her daughter-in-law.

Grant had been by the ICU several times that day. He'd had two new admissions, two pneumothorax patients, and had about ten others who were there for various problems, mostly related to acute exacerbations of chronic bronchitis.

On Monday night, she'd texted Grant that she wanted him. He'd been on her doorstep in less than an hour and brought her to even higher planes than he had over the weekend.

On Tuesday night, after she'd come home from her mother's, she'd wanted to text him, but had denied herself the pleasure, not wanting to do two nights in a row. Two nights in a row seemed too relationshippy. She hadn't technically listed that as a rule, but she should have. Sex with Grant two nights in a row would just be…fun, wonderful, exactly what she wanted. Which was why she had settled with just texting a "Not tonite" in response to his "Can I C U?". Which made her irritable because she wanted him.

What was that Scarlett O'Hara had once said about tomorrow? About it being another day? Well, tomorrow couldn't arrive fast enough for Joni.

* * *

Adrenaline rushing through his veins, Grant slid the tube down his patient's throat, intubating the woman and hooking her to the artificial life support that would keep her breathing. He ran through his checklist to make sure placement was correct, and watched her chest rise and fall with the aid of the ventilator.

The forty-year-old woman had gone into acute respiratory failure when she'd overdosed on her prescription pain medications mixed with alcohol. He'd seen it happen before. Someone in pain popped another pill, took a drink or two, thinking it wouldn't hurt even though they weren't supposed to mix their medications with alcohol, thinking that the combination would ease the ache or at least make them not care.

He'd seen it happen with Ashley, had watched her destroy her life, the life they'd had together, almost destroying him too.

Kathy Conner hadn't cared about much of anything when she'd drifted into sleep and her husband hadn't been able to wake her. Grant felt sorry for the man, felt thankful he had finally extricated himself from Ashley's messed-up life.

"Great job," the emergency room physician praised. Grant had been paged to assist when the woman had lapsed into acute respiratory failure minutes after arriving at the emergency department via ambulance.

"I was afraid we wouldn't be able to save this one," the emergency physician continued, pulling off his latex gloves.

"She's not out of the water yet." Unfortunately.

Just because her breathing had stabilized with the aid of the ventilator, it didn't fool Grant. The woman had suppressed her central nervous system to the point her body functions could shut down at any point. She'd be lucky if she only needed a ventilator to keep her alive. Just as easily her liver or kidneys could fail from the toxins she'd poisoned her body with.

How many times had he watched over Ashley as she'd detoxed, praying that she pulled through? He glanced at his patient, a mixture of disgust and pity filling him. With so many of his patients fighting for every breath, he sometimes struggled to remain compassionate with someone who treated life so carelessly.

"Call ICU and have them get a bed ready," Grant told the nurse who'd been assisting with the procedure. "Ms. Conner is going to need close care over the next twenty-four hours to see her through this one. I'm going to talk to her husband and let him know what's going on, then I've got to see the patients at my office. If anything changes, have me paged."

When Grant finally made it to the ICU wing, the first person he saw was Joni. Instantly, his body tightened. Instantly, he had flashbacks to the previous night. To every other night for the past five weeks.

Why she only called him every other night he could only imagine, and did, but on "their night" she didn't hesitate or dawdle. She called, told him exactly what she wanted, and he came running.

Not exactly what he'd had in mind when he'd agreed to her rules. He wanted more than the hours they spent in bed. Because essentially he was her booty call.

Sure, while they were together, she gave him her all, holding nothing back, letting him hold her afterwards until oftentimes he grew hard again and had to have her a second or third time.

Sure, she laughed and played with him in bed, answered most questions he asked—no, she wasn't allergic to flowers and, yes, she was on a diet, because, *duh*, what woman wasn't perpetually on a diet?—but at no point did she seem interested in changing the status quo of their relationship. At no point would she answer any question about her childhood or her parents or about how she occupied her time on the nights they didn't see each other.

What did she do on the nights she wasn't with him? Who was she with? He didn't believe there was someone else, but he couldn't shake the feeling that on the nights Joni wasn't with him, she was doing something he wouldn't like.

Then again, only five weeks had passed. Maybe he should stick to what he'd told Mrs. Sain. Give Joni time. Or maybe he should try some of the older woman's other suggestions, see how those panned out for him. Flowers, chocolates, or one of those fairy figures he'd noticed around her house.

What woman who collected figurines of such whimsical creatures only wanted a physical relationship with a man? Surely she was a romantic at heart? Surely he just needed to appeal to that love of fantasy and convince her that she should trust in the chemistry between them?

At that moment, she glanced up, saw him. Her full lips began to curve into a smile, but then she caught herself, sobered, and glanced away.

Smiling at him at work was against the rules.

He'd had enough of her rules, enough of her shutting him out, enough of not knowing what she did every other night that she didn't want him to know about.

It was time to break out Plan B.

Let the wooing begin.

Joni came out of her patient room and caught sight of Grant standing near the nurses' station.

His head was thrown back and he was laughing at something Samantha had said.

A pang of jealousy shot through her. Red-hot jealousy.

Her entire insides had lit up like a Christmas tree when she'd spotted him earlier in the day. It had been all she could do not to drop everything she was doing and run to him, wrap her arms around him, and tell him how wonderful he looked.

It had taken all her willpower to rein in how he affected her, to damp down her happiness at seeing him, and remain professionally detached.

He hadn't seemed to mind. He'd walked right past her without saying a single word, without an accidental brush against her or even another glance her way, as far as she knew.

But what could she say? She'd been the one to tell him to ignore her at work, that theirs was a sex-only relationship. He'd been true to his promise.

Just because she was feeling the constraints she'd put on them, it didn't mean she'd been wrong to put them there. Just the opposite. If him ignoring her bothered her this much, she'd been right to keep as much distance between them as possible in her professional life.

If every night she wanted to call him, beg him to come to her, stay with her, then she'd been right to keep their trysts to every other night, to insist he couldn't stay until morning.

Her rules might be a pain in the kisser, but if she wanted to walk away without having to clean up a mess she didn't need, then she had to cling to them, had to make him stick to them.

No problem there. He seemed just fine with their affair the way it was. What did he do on his off night? She never asked and he never told. Sure, he texted her one-liners meant to make her smile—or ache with desire—but he could send those from anywhere.

Even from another woman's bed.

She grimaced. No, Grant wasn't spending time in another woman's bed.

Was he?

Before she could think better of it, she marched over to where he stood.

Enjoying the surprised look on his face a bit too

much, she grabbed hold of his scrub top and led him away from the nurses' station, away from a laughing Samantha. But where to?

"Not a word," she ordered when she opened the door to the supply closet and he opened his mouth. "Not a single word about where we are."

Instead he flashed his most wicked smile, shrugged, and didn't utter a single word.

"I forgot to tell you a very important rule."

His brow arched, but he didn't speak, his silence forcing her to go on.

She gulped, then lifted her chin. "While we are involved, neither of us can have sex with anyone else. We're monogamous or not at all."

His eyes widened with surprise, then twinkled with amusement. "I never took you for the jealous type."

"Who said you could talk?" she snapped back, hating it that he read her so clearly.

He grinned. "I have to tell you, I never took you for the bossy type either, but I'm liking it. Liking it a lot."

She rolled her eyes. "I'm not bossy."

"Lady, you are a total control freak, but I'm crazy about you anyway."

"I am not a—" The rest of what he'd said hit her. "You're crazy about me?"

"You think these past few weeks have just been about sex?"

She bit her lip, hard. She needed the pain to dull the euphoria blossoming within her at his words.

No. No. No.

"The past few weeks have just been about sex. Don't say things like you are crazy about me."

He snorted softly, pulled her to him. "If you insist. I won't tell you how crazy I am about you or how good you feel."

Wow, but he felt good pressed against her, too.

"I insist."

"Fine, but for the record we are in the supply closet." His head lowered to within centimeters of hers. "I distinctly recall us discussing this."

Butterflies danced in her belly. "We are at work, Grant."

"We are in a supply closet. Alone." He said the last with great emphasis. "You're mine."

His lips covered hers.

How could she deny him when he was right? They were in a supply closet. Alone.

Joni's face burned hot when Samantha didn't bother covering her laughter. Had her friend been laughing the entire time? Or just had a fresh bout hit her?

"Did I really just see you come out of the supply closet?" Samantha snorted.

Best friends were like that. Thought they had the right to point out the obvious and laugh about it, too.

Joni ignored her friend's laughter and smoothed her wrinkled scrub top. Not that she hadn't straightened the material a dozen times prior to stepping out of the closet. But each time she had, Grant had pulled her back to him and kissed her again.

When he'd slipped his hand under her scrub top and cupped her breast through her bra she'd known she was in danger of pushing Grant against the shelving and having her way with him. She'd wanted to do just that.

Had she lost her mind?

Anyone could have opened that door and caught them. Then what? Would she have been called into the nursing director's office and reprimanded? Would she have been handed her walking papers for inappropriate behavior? Her behavior was inappropriate. She was on the clock, had patients depending on her.

Her behavior was everything Mark had falsely accused her of. Everything she'd had to defend her job and nursing license for. Well, except for the under-the-influence part. She never drank or did any kind of drug. Never had and never would. Too risky.

Needing to escape, she'd run out of the closet, leaving a startled Grant behind her.

"I needed supplies," she explained to her friend, despite the fact she'd come out of the closet breathless and empty-handed.

"Ha." Samantha's gaze went past Joni to where Grant was now stepping out of the closet. "I see exactly what you needed. He must have worked up a sweat helping you find those supplies."

They both watched him disappear into Kathy Conner's room. An odd tug pulled at Joni's heart.

Despite all the reasons she shouldn't have been in that closet, she couldn't blame him. She'd been the one to drag him there. It wasn't as if he hadn't warned her about being alone in the supply closet. Had she been tempting fate? Tempting him because she'd been jealous at the thought of him possibly being with someone other than her?

"It's not like that." It was exactly like that. Both in regard to what her friend meant and to her own treacherous thoughts.

"No?" Samantha sighed. "Well, it should be. How many times do I have to tell you that your rules are the craziest things I've ever heard?"

"They're not crazy." The supply-closet incident proved that. Had she stuck to her rules she wouldn't have just risked throwing her career away. Wouldn't be feeling jealousy over a man she was only having a short-term affair with. "You don't understand."

"Then make me understand," Samantha urged. "Because you're right. I don't understand why you have a wonderful man like Grant who is nuts about you and you're holding him at arm's length and refusing to let him in."

Ha. The reason Grant was nuts about her was because they weren't real. Men wanted what they couldn't have.

"Of all the people in the world, you shouldn't be accusing me of not letting him in. Not with the way you keep refusing Vann. I let Grant in."

"Yeah, you let him in all right." Samantha slammed the medication cart drawer closed with more force than necessary. "Every other night you let him in. Then you kick him back to the curb."

Joni winced at her friend's crass words. "Sleeping with him every night would feel too much like a relationship."

Samantha rolled her eyes. "Call it whatever you like, but for you to sleep with a man at all is a relationship, Joni. We both know you aren't a one-night-stand kind of girl."

"You're right." She lifted her chin. "We've had a lot more than just one night."

"And you have a lot more between you than just sex. Admit it."

"No."

"Well, don't look now, but your boy toy is finished in Mrs. Conner's room and is headed this way," Samantha warned. "Better go hide in the break room if you want to maintain your pretense of not having a real relationship with him."

Joni shook her head, but did as her friend suggested and ducked into the break room. She stopped short just inside the doorway.

A square box about the size of a coffee mug sat on the break-room table with a ribbon tied around it and a card propped beside it. "Joni" was written across the envelope in dark nondescript calligraphy.

Had Samantha done this?

Her friend knew she'd been emotionally up and down over the past few weeks. High over how happy she was when she was with Grant. Tense over how much she missed him and thought of him when they weren't together.

Not quite sure what to think, or even what she wanted to think, she picked up the box. Not very heavy, but definitely something inside.

She started to gently shake the box, but an inner voice warned her not to.

Instead, she untied the ribbon and lifted the lid.

A cupcake.

A single beautifully frosted red-velvet cupcake. Its decadent scent wafted from the box and made her breathe in.

Unable to resist, she dipped her fingertip into the icing and licked off the sweet confection. Rich cream-cheese icing melted in her mouth, delighting her taste buds and sending her into sensation overload.

Mmm, but she was going to kill Samantha for doing this.

Getting naked with a man as beautiful as Grant had left her wondering how he could possibly find her desirable when there was nothing tight or sculpted about her body. Samantha knew that, knew she was trying to lose a few pounds, that on the nights she wasn't doing the horizontal mumbo-jumbo with Grant she was sweating to the oldies and every other torturous exercise DVD she'd ever bought but rarely used until three weeks ago. Now she did AA with her mother, then she did FF, Flab to Fab.

Deciding that one more small dollop of icing wouldn't hurt, she stuck her finger into her mouth, sucked the sugary treat off, then tore open the card.

Because a woman as beautiful as you should never diet

Not from Samantha.

From her Secret Admirer. Ha. Right.

CHAPTER NINE

Joni lay in her bed, beneath her bunched around her comforter. Through the darkness, she stared at the lit screen as she typed her message.

I know what you did today, she wrote.

What's that?

She smiled. Don't play dumb with me.

Playing dumb is not what I want to do with you.

A giggle escaped her lips as she typed her response. Your secret admirer fooled no one.

I have no idea what you are referring to.

Sure you don't.

Is there something you should tell me?

Thank you, but don't let it happen again.

She closed her eyes, anticipating the vibration of her phone signaling that he'd messaged back. When the buzz shook her hand, giddiness whipped through her. She punched the button to display his message. A thousand fighter jets took flight in her belly as she read what he'd written.

Invite me over so you can thank me properly for whatever it is you're giving me credit for doing.

She wanted to. Desperately she wanted to invite him over and feel the onslaught of sensations just being with him always gave her. To feel the pleasure of having all his attention focused on her, on bringing her body to as high as it would go time and again.

I can't.

He made her wait a full minute in the darkness before her phone jarred against her fingers.

You mean you won't.

Same difference.

Hardly.

His disappointment was palpable, made her second-guess her resolve to stick to not being with him two nights in a row. She wanted him so much. Would welcoming him into her bed tonight really be that much of a problem?

The fact she was questioning her resolve said, yes, it would. Sort of like when an alcoholic thought they could have just one drink.

Her phone shook again, startling her as she hadn't yet responded to his text.

Actually, not hard isn't accurate. Tell me what you'd do to thank me if I was there.

Oh, my, she thought, more turned on by his request than she would have believed possible.

What? You want phone gratitude?

Amongst other things.

Excitement surged deep inside her.

You admitting your guilt?

I'm admitting nothing. Now thank me.

Smiling, Joni closed her eyes, let her mind wander. If he were there, if she could thank him any way she liked, what would she do?

I'd take what was left of this naughtily delicious cupcake and I'd smear the icing down your chest.

In her mind she was doing just that, spreading the icing down the groove that cut his six pack in two. She wouldn't lift her finger until she'd left an icing trail all the way down to where his own happy trail disappeared. She loved his chest, loved that happy trail.

Sounds messy. Then what?

Messy? Ha, she'd give him messy. She could

picture him lying in his bed, phone in hand, grinning as he'd typed his message.

I'd clean up the mess I made.

Oh, really?

Oh, definitely.

In her mind she already was.

How?

With my tongue.

Through the miles and darkness separating them, she heard him moan when he read her message.

Tell me more, cupcake.

Cupcake? She'd never been into nicknames, but she didn't correct him, just let warmth fill her as she thought about what "more" she wanted to tell him. She closed her eyes, pictured him standing beside her bed, icing streaked down his chest and abdomen. She imagined herself next to him, bent to where her mouth connected with his skin just so. Mmm… Had he heard her moan as she'd heard his?

I'd clean the icing off with little licks, savoring each burst of flavor as the icing melted on my tongue.

You're killing me here, came shooting back immediately.

She giggled in a way too feminine way and punched her reply. It's called cleaning, not killing.

Silence, then, What would you do next?

Smiling, she closed her eyes again, let her mind go back to their fantasy.

Well, it would take me a while to clean all that icing off, to make sure I didn't leave any stickiness. I like to do a thorough job at anything I do, you know.

I know. Had he just gulped?

I might have gotten some in your navel that would require a lot of tongue action.

Might.

Would be hard work, she teased.

Very hard. But someone has to do it, right?

Right.

What's next?

Next? What was next? If she'd just licked cake icing off Grant's body, what would she do next if he was at her mercy?

Next would be your turn.

I get to rub icing on you and lick it off?

If that's what you want, cupcake. She wasn't sure why she tossed the endearment back at him, but doing so felt right, fun.

I want you, Joni.

I want you, too, Grant.

That an invitation?

Was it?

I… She hesitated, deleted the lone letter and started over. Nite, Grant.

For the longest time she waited for his response. She was just this side of asleep when it finally came, the vibration of her phone startling her awake.

She pushed the button that lit her screen, touched the text icon, and read his message.

Rules are meant to be broken, cupcake. Dream of me.

After way too long, she fell asleep and did just that.

Joni pulled the sticky note off her driver-side window and shook her head at the message. If you could call it that. A hand-drawn smiley face was the only thing on the yellow paper, but had the note contained words of poetry the gesture couldn't have touched her heart more.

She supposed she should be upset about all the little things Grant kept doing. A donut with the word "smile" written in icing. A handful of daisies that just very well may have been picked off the side of the road and left on her doorstep. All sorts of silly little things left at work with a card from her secret admirer.

He'd agreed to her terms. He'd just found a sneaky way around them. He still hadn't admitted that any of the gifts were from him. But she knew.

As did Samantha and several other of her coworkers who had started teasing about all her secret-admirer gifts.

Were they all in on his "secret admirer" act? Helping him pull off the little things he did? Helping him come up with just the right thing to say or do to put a giddy, happy feeling in her chest? To set off fireworks in her belly?

No, she shouldn't be smiling as she pulled the

smiley sticky off her car window, but that didn't stop her.

Grant made her smile. A lot.

Hand on the doorhandle, she paused, closed her eyes and let images of Grant into her mind. The man felt so perfect.

"You waiting on someone?" a male voice whispered close to her ear.

"Just you," she replied, spinning to face him and almost wrapping her arms around his neck before she recalled where they were. Since the supply-closet debacle they'd pretty much stuck to their "no touching at the hospital" policy, not that she believed they were fooling anyone these days. "Aren't you in the wrong parking lot?"

"Not if this is where you are." His smile warmed her heart, but tension lines marred his expression. "I meant to catch you earlier to find out what time you wanted me over, but I got hung up with Kathy Conner."

Kathy Conner. Joni had spent a lot of time talking with her husband, her teenage son, had given them information on addiction. How could she not have? The woman reminded her of her mother, of sitting in a hospital waiting room not knowing if perhaps this was the time her mother wouldn't be coming home. The nurses she'd met during her mother's overdose hospital stays had influenced her so much and for that she was grateful, wanted to be a positive influence on others.

"I heard she had to be sedated to keep from pulling out her vent tube."

He nodded. "The woman is damned lucky to be alive. She should be ashamed to put her family through this."

Joni cringed at the brusqueness in Grant's voice. "Addiction is a disease, not something someone does because they want to be cruel to their loved ones. She obviously has a lot of problems." She hoped Kathy Conner pulled her life together the way Joni's mother had. Not that the fear of relapse wasn't always present. Each and every sober day was a blessing not to be taken lightly, and Joni didn't. That was why she was so diligent in attending AA with her mother, in her visits to watch for the slightest sign of trouble.

"Obviously."

The bitter way Grant said the words struck Joni as wrong, very unGrant-like. The man had more compassion and heart for his patients than any doctor she'd ever worked with. But she hadn't imagined his earlier brusqueness. His comment had sounded judgmental, lacking in empathy.

"Not everyone's life is cut and dried. You don't know what pushed her down the path she's chosen, what she's dealt with."

"You're right." He didn't meet her eyes.

Warning bells blared. She didn't know why it was so important that Grant not be judgmental the way Mark had, but it was. They were only short term, physical. What he thought didn't matter.

Yet it did matter.

"You don't really believe that, do you?"

He sighed, glanced around the parking lot, raked his fingers through his thick hair. "I believe we shouldn't be having this discussion, because we obviously disagree."

"Obviously." She mimicked his earlier comment with a hefty dose of sarcasm. She knew she was out of line, yet she couldn't contain herself.

Couldn't ignore that his quick-to-judge attitude bothered her. "So, if I was like Kathy Conner, you'd not want me any more?"

His face paled. Visibly blanched so white she thought he might pass out. "That isn't funny, Joni."

"My question wasn't meant to be funny. It was meant to glean information."

"You aren't an addict, so it's irrelevant."

"For all you know, I could be."

"Are you?" he asked from between gritted teeth.

"No, I'm not." But wasn't that her greatest fear? That she'd end up becoming what Mark had told the nursing director she was—an addict? "Does whether I am or not matter? We're sex only. Would sleeping with me not be as good if I had problems? Or would you be sleeping with someone else? Heather Abellano perhaps? Or maybe you already want to be sleeping with her and that's what this is about?"

He worked his jaw back and forth. "I agreed to your rules, one of which included that while we were together I wouldn't be with another woman.

Not that you had to put that rule into effect anyway. If I wanted to be with another woman I'd end things with you and be with another woman."

Her heart balled up into a tight lump in her chest.

"Is that what you're doing?" Why did she feel like she couldn't breathe? "If so, just get it over with so I can go home."

Go home and cry her eyes out. Hadn't she just minutes before been musing about how happy she was? Ha, she should have known better.

Color splashed his cheeks and his eyes burned blue fire. "Why do you always jump to the worst conclusions where I am concerned?"

"I don't," she denied, fighting tears and failing.

"Yes, you do." Although he kept his volume to a minimum, anger laced his words. "You assumed I'd slept with the women on my golf team, that I sleep around, period, that I want to sleep with Dr. Abellano's daughter. Have I done something that makes you feel I deserve those assumptions?"

Had he? No, Mark had, but she didn't want to discuss Mark.

"Silence," he pointed out. "Which means you just don't want to tell me what the real issues are or you're just waiting for me to slip up so you can point out my many flaws and walk away. Is that it?"

"I don't want you to slip up." Not to mention that she wasn't even sure he had flaws. The man was too perfect. Maybe that was his flaw. Perfection.

"No?"

She shook her head. She didn't.

"But you expect me to?"

He was right. She did expect him to fall off his pedestal, to do something so wrong that her heart would break. She knew he would. It was just a matter of time. Wasn't that why she'd had to have her rules to begin with? So that when things went wrong she had an insurance policy to protect her heart? So she wouldn't let him become tangled with thoughts of the future?

But she didn't want things to end. Not yet.

"I have done this your way, Joni, even though I didn't agree with the sex-only relationship, not that it ever really was sex only for either of us. I thought if I did things your way for long enough, you'd realize I was sincere, that I wanted a real relationship with you, that I want you as part of my life. But I'm wasting my time, aren't I?"

No, she wanted to cry, he wasn't wasting his time. But she'd only be delaying the inevitable. If he stayed, then what? They'd carry on until he realized she came from a messed-up home, until he judged her mother the way he'd judged Kathy Conner? Would she be lessened in his eyes because she was the daughter of an addict? Because she'd never turn her back on her mother?

"You can't even deny it, can you?" He sounded disgusted. She supposed he was. "Is this what you want, Joni?"

How could she answer? She wasn't even sure what he was asking. "Is what what I want?"

"To call an end to this pretense we have going?"

Pretense? Emotions she refused to label shriveled up and died inside her. She should cut her losses now. The fact she was crying already implied she was more tangled up with him than she should be.

"That would probably be for the best." Embarrassed at the moisture in her eyes, on her cheeks, she met his narrowed gaze head on, hoping she looked tougher than she felt. "But, no, I don't want us to end."

He swore under his breath, took her hands into his. "Tell me what you want and, if I can, I'll give it to you."

What did she want? Great question. One she wished she knew the answer to. All she knew was that she wasn't ready to let him go.

"I want you," she answered honestly, wondering if he could feel how her body shook. "I want you to kiss me until I forget everything, except you."

Grant wanted to scream. Really? He was trying to have a serious conversation with her, to talk about his feelings, and she wanted to bring everything back to physical? Weren't women supposed to want to talk about their feelings? Not his Joni.

"Here?" he asked, testing her and knowing that was what he did. They stood in the employee parking lot. Anyone could see them. Was she ready to acknowledge what was between them?

Grimacing slightly, she shook her head. "You know not here."

Oh, he knew all right. He knew a lot of things. Like that her friends, even Samantha, knew very little about her past, knew very little about what made her tick. Joni had secrets. A lot of secrets, and she wanted to keep it that way.

The question was, why? What was she hiding? Not what Ashley had so effectively hidden during the first year of their relationship. Joni had said she wasn't an addict. Had she seen how he'd been unable to breathe while he'd waited for her answer? Had she seen the relief wash over him at her denial? But the facts didn't quite add up.

After years of dealing with Ashley's drug problem, he'd done his research before asking Joni out. No one had raised any concerns. Right or wrong, he'd even taken a peek at her employee file, had seen her repeated negative random drug screens. He'd thought he'd been smart, had taken precautions. But she was hiding something.

"Why don't you want me to kiss you right now?"

Her glassy eyes widened. "It's inappropriate and asking for problems."

"Because?"

She glanced away, took too long considering her reply. "There are things you don't know."

Exactly. There were a lot of things he didn't know. Mysteries he'd like to unravel.

"Such as?" he pushed.

But rather than open up to him, she shook her head. "Doesn't matter."

He wanted to throw his hands into the air. "You're wrong. Everything about you matters." Despite her rules against touch, he bent enough to kiss her forehead. "You matter, Joni."

Her big green eyes met his in challenge. "Because of sex?"

Had a more frustrating woman ever existed?

"If that's what you want to believe, fine, because of sex." Was that all they'd ever have? Sex? He wanted so much more, wanted her to be his. The thought that she might completely shut him out someday had him wrapping his arms around her, hating it that she stiffened against him, knowing that if he wanted to keep Joni in his life, patience was the name of the game.

Unfortunately he was feeling more and more frustrated and less and less patient.

Grant had planned the day down to a *T*. He and Joni were going to have a real date, spend time together without it revolving around sex.

Not that he didn't like the sex. What wasn't to like about Joni's hunger, which matched his own? About the way his body shredded into a million bits when he came inside her?

But he hadn't started their relationship wanting just sex. He wanted Joni. All of her. Not just her body.

Since she insisted on abiding by her Rules of Affair, as he'd dubbed them, today was his one chance to prove that they would be good together outside the physical realm.

Their hot-air balloon trip. Their first "real" date. Their only "real" date, according to Joni.

He'd had to think outside the box to come up with something to give her since flowers were out of the question. The hot-air balloon refrigerator magnet was corny, but he wasn't allowed to give a more traditional gift. He figured she'd put it on her refrigerator, would hopefully smile and think of him when she saw it.

Truth was, he liked coming up with the silly little things he did for Joni. Because he wanted to make her smile, wanted to brighten her day.

Because he was crazy about her.

He knocked on her front door. Checking his watch, he was glad to see they had plenty of time, could maybe do some sightseeing before arriving at Skyline.

"Come on in," she called from somewhere in her house.

He twisted the knob and went to find her so they could leave. He'd barely gotten the front door shut when he spotted her. His heart fell to his knees and another body part rose to the occasion.

Naked as the day she was born except for a pair of red high heels and a stethoscope dangling around her neck, Joni stood just a few feet inside the doorway. She had obviously been hiding behind the door as he entered her house so he could get the full effect of her outfit—or lack thereof.

"Morning," she offered, her voice low and husky. "Wanna play doctor with me?"

Seeing her always caused a testosterone surge through his veins, but her greeting him wearing nothing but her birthday suit, heels, and a stethoscope? Lord help him. Today was not supposed to be about sex.

"Joni." His jaw hung somewhere near his ankles. Unable to tear his gaze away from the beauty of her exposed body, he held up his wrist and pointed to his watch. "We need to go."

Today was about building a foundation for their relationship. One that didn't involve him playing doctor with his favorite nurse.

"Our flight," he reminded her. His gaze traveled over her. His nostrils flared. His pulse thumped a heavy rapid beat at his throat.

"Come here." She beckoned him to her. "I need to check your heart rate."

His heart rate was on the rise. He would like to think he was strong enough to stick to his plan, to resist the pull of her body for at least a day. Obviously, he wasn't.

When Joni crooked her finger, he was a goner. "To hell with our flight."

Hands were everywhere. Mouths were everywhere.

He quickly ended up inside her against her living-room wall, on her sofa, in the middle of the hallway floor because somehow they hadn't made it all the way to her bedroom.

So much for keeping his hands to himself.

Okay, so technically Joni wasn't supposed to go on a date with Grant, but she had sort of promised that she would go if he won the hot-air balloon package, hadn't she?

So here she was, in the front seat of a gas-guzzling monster of a vehicle headed out on their late-afternoon adventure. Even sitting here next to him was an adventure. Mostly because every now and then he'd look over at her and give her that grin. The knock her off her feet he was so gorgeous, grin.

Going out with him like this was against the

rules she'd set up to keep her heart safe, but just so long as she remembered that none of this was real, all the closeness and smiles and attraction was an illusion, here today and gone tomorrow, she'd be fine. Really, she would.

So just for today she was going to relax and enjoy being with this man who stole her breath with just a half-cocked smile.

"What are you thinking?"

She cut her gaze to him, her breath catching in her throat. The way he looked at her had made her feel like the most beautiful girl in the world.

"About how much fun we are going to have today."

He flashed a naughty grin and waggled his brows. "Don't know about you, but I already had some fun today." His eyes twinkling with merriment, he drew his brows together. "Let me rephrase that. I do know about you. Lots about you. We both already had some fun today."

He was right. They had both had fun.

Because the second he'd stepped into her house his clothes had begun flying every which way in a frenzied strip-fest. She leaned back against the

Hummer's passenger seat, relived the memories. Oh, yeah, they'd had fun.

Hot, sweaty, orgasmic fun.

Just remembering had her shifting in her seat, her panties dampening between her legs. Again. How did he do that? Make her so physically aware of him? Make her want him so much?

She'd never considered herself an overly sexual person—if anything, quite the opposite. But with Grant she couldn't get enough.

"I recognize that look," he warned from the driver's seat.

This time she was the one flashing a naughty grin. "What look would that be?"

"Uh-uh, not again, Joni Thompson." He winced, shook his head as if to clear his thoughts. "I can't believe I'm saying that, that I'm not pulling off the road and giving you exactly what you want, but we don't have time. Not after this morning." He took a deep breath, met her eyes for a brief moment. "I want to take this balloon ride with you."

She sighed with great exaggeration. If she pushed even slightly, he would pull off the road.

The realization was quite heady and a big turn-on. She wanted him.

"Get those thoughts out of your head."

She smiled, not bothering to mask her thoughts, not bothering to pretend she couldn't see exactly the effect her thoughts were having on him. She liked the effect she had on him. He made her feel beautiful, sexy, as if looking on her body was a cherished gift. When he looked at her she could see the desire in his eyes.

For whatever crazy wonderful reason, Grant wanted her.

Sure, it wasn't happily-ever-after, but since they were just physical, what did that matter? She didn't want happily-ever-after. She wanted Grant. She was going to ride this gravy train for all it was worth. Ride him for all she was worth until the attraction between them played out.

She twisted in her seat so she could more readily see him. Reaching out, she traced her finger down the clingy blue cotton of his T-shirt, lower and lower until she hit the waistband of his jeans.

His very tight jeans.

"Joni," he groaned. "Don't."

"Don't what?" She almost moaned at the pleasure hidden away behind the faded denim. The
man did amazing things for a pair of jeans. But
what he did when he was out of those jeans…
wow was all she could think to describe how his
body felt inside hers. Wow. Wow. Wow.

Her fingers toyed at his waistband, dipped into
his navel, undid his snap.

"Joni." Her name came out half warning, half
moan.

"What? You don't think you're up for a quickie?"
she teased.

"Oh, I'm definitely up for a quickie." The bulge
behind his zipper left no doubt. "Only problem
is we have to be at Skyline in thirty minutes or
we might miss our ride."

She scraped her nails over where his jeans
strained. "Might be worth it."

"I'm sure it would be," he rushed out. "You always are. But I'm not pulling over."

"Who said anything about pulling over?"

With a daring she hadn't possessed prior to
him, she unhooked her seat belt, shifted in her
seat, and lifted the hem of her T-shirt, exposing

a new silk and lace bra showcasing her heavy breasts.

He'd watched her dress when they'd finished that morning, had commented on how fantastic she looked in her underwear and how just looking at her made him want to take them off her again.

"Joni," he groaned, not taking his eyes off the road. She knew he could see her in his peripheral vision, though. The way he white-knuckled the steering-wheel was proof enough.

Knowing he was attuned to her every movement, she knelt on the floor of the vehicle and kissed where her hand had been moments before.

His abdominal muscles clenched against his T-shirt, his tension palpable as she ran her hands over him, down his muscular thighs. He made a noise that sounded like more of a growl than a word.

"Hmm?" she murmured as she struggled with his zipper, finally parting his jeans. She lowered her face, nuzzling against the soft cotton of his boxer briefs, breathing in his musky scent.

The man gave off some serious pheromones.

Just the smell of his body made her want to rip

off his clothes and drag him between the seats so she could lick him all over.

Actually, she was going to lick and have her way with him right now. Without him pulling over.

With his hands occupied on the steering-wheel, she could explore his body without getting distracted by what he was doing to her body. Normally, if she was touching him, he was touching back. She'd soon lose all thought except…well, the man was turning her into a sex fiend.

"I should have tied you to your seat."

She laughed, glancing up at his handsome face. "I can think of a few things I'd like you to do to me if I were tied to the seat."

He audibly swallowed, placed his hand over hers on his thigh, keeping her palm locked against him. "You drive me crazy."

"You want me to stop?" She pressed her lips to where the tip of him jutted out of the top of his underwear.

"Yes." He gritted his teeth together when she licked him.

"Yes, you want me to stop?" She ran her tongue along the groove of his head, now fully exposed.

"No," he growled, his knuckles popping he gripped the steering-wheel so tightly. "I don't want you to stop, Joni. Not ever."

The need in his voice about undid her, made her want to give him pleasure, lots of pleasure.

"Good, 'cause I didn't plan to." She shoved his underwear out of her way, exposing the hard length of him, and didn't stop.

Not when he cursed and drove the Hummer off the road to a quick stop.

Not when he buried his hands in her hair, urging her on, telling her how amazing she made him feel and how he wanted to be inside her.

Not when he cried out her name and exploded.

CHAPTER TEN

TAKING a deep breath of fresh mountain air, Grant squeezed Joni's hand, lifted it to his lips and kissed her fingertips.

Her eyes bright, she smiled at him.

God, he loved her smile, loved doing things he knew would put a smile on her face.

"This is amazing." She gestured to the view beyond the hot-air balloon basket they floated in high above the ground. "Thank you for bringing me."

He agreed that the view of the mountains in the distance was spectacular, but she was amazing. Completely and totally amazing.

Everything about her. The way she cared for her patients, the way her eyes would meet his and he'd know exactly what she was thinking without either of them speaking a word, the way she came around him without holding back and felt so perfect in his arms afterwards.

The way she pushed him over the brink time and again, making him go a little crazy with need for her.

The only thing that wasn't amazing was her ridiculous rules.

Which she reminded him of quite frequently.

When she refused to actually go out on a date with him.

When she made him go home in the middle of the night because she didn't want to wake up beside him.

When she refused to tell him what she did on the nights they weren't together, even acted oddly when he asked, as if whatever she was doing, she didn't want him to know.

When she refused to acknowledge to anyone that she was his despite the fact that they weren't fooling anyone who knew them.

She was his. In every sense of the word, Joni belonged to him.

Only she refused to admit it. Refused to acknowledge that there was something very special between the two of them.

Only sex, she'd say. Only chemistry, she'd insist. Only physical, she'd explain. He'd had sex before. He'd had chemistry before. He'd had only physical before.

Joni wasn't only anything.

She was everything.

Only she wouldn't allow him inside the wall she'd erected. A wall full of rules and regulations meant to keep distance between them.

He wanted more.

Had always wanted more with her, he realized.

Only every time he tried to make their relationship about something more than physical attraction, she'd either spout rules at him or blindside him with lust and he'd end up inside her.

Not that he was complaining. They were phenomenal together. Their bodies were so in tune with each other. But today was his chance to show her how other aspects of their lives would merge just as well, that they weren't just about physical pleasure.

Not that he was doing such a great job proving a thing. They'd had sex at her place, and then again in his Hummer.

Or did his pit stop even count as sex as she hadn't got to orgasm?

He'd been intent on keeping his eyes on the road, on not letting her get to him. Then he'd glanced over, seen her creamy cleavage on display beneath that lacy concoction she called a bra. He'd about busted free of his jeans. He'd been a goner before she'd ever put her plump lips against him and had no idea how he'd lasted the few minutes he had.

Never had he felt so out of control of his own body. Only with Joni.

"You're thinking about the Hummer, aren't you?" she asked close to his ear so the balloonist couldn't hear.

"It's not my vehicle I'm thinking of."

She giggled, looking happy. Really happy. More than anything he wanted her to hang onto that feeling. Wanted to be the one to give her that feeling, to make her happy.

Because he'd begun to suspect Joni hadn't had a happy life. That something or someone had hurt her and caused her to think she needed all those rigid rules.

"I want to date you. For us to be real in every sense. For the world to know that you are mine, Joni, because I think I'm falling in love with you." Where the words came from, he didn't know. Only that he couldn't take them back, neither could he deny them.

Had he wanted to kill her happiness, he'd achieved it in spades.

She stepped away from him, glancing desperately around them, over the basket edge, obviously needing space, much more space than the balloon basket offered.

Much more than the vast open sky around them offered.

For a brief, scary moment he thought she considered bailing out of the basket despite the hundreds of feet they floated above the ground.

He stepped closer, reached for her, but she shook her head.

"Don't say that." She wrapped her arms around herself, rubbed her palms back and forth over her upper arms as if she were cold. Maybe she was.

Maybe he was a fool.

Taking a deep breath, he handed her the jacket they'd been instructed to bring. "Here, put this on and forget I said anything."

Not that he would be able to forget.

"Joni?" he prompted, when she didn't take the light coat he held out.

Without glancing at him, she slipped the jacket on.

Then she stood there, looking lost, as if she didn't know what she was supposed to do next, as if she were trapped in this balloon with him and was afraid.

He hadn't meant to say what he had, but he couldn't take back his words, couldn't erase them. But today was his day, the day she'd promised him on the night they'd first made love, and she owed him this chance.

"Come here."

She hesitated.

"Come here, Joni."

Head down, she did. He wrapped his arms around her, held her close, kissed the top of her head. He repositioned her to where she was close to the edge of the basket, her back pressed tightly against his front, and he wrapped his arms around her. She remained stiff in his arms, and he bit back a sigh. He held her close, breathing in her sweet jasmine scent. Together they took in the beautiful scenery around them. Slowly, she relaxed against him and began pointing out different things below them.

Fine, he would play by her rules for a little while longer. Whether he liked them or not.

Joni smiled at the man who handed her a glass of champagne. Champagne. Ha.

He'd said he thought he was falling in love with her.

Not the most flattering of declarations.

Not even a confident one.

How could Grant be falling in love with her when their relationship was only based on physical fulfillment? When he didn't even know her or else he would never have handed her the champagne?

Besides, he couldn't be falling in love with her.

Because if he was then that meant her rules didn't offer protection and she could be falling in love with him too. No way would she allow that to happen.

No way would she risk such pain and humiliation again.

If it was happening, she'd have to change her rules pronto. Would have to add a rule that they couldn't see each other any more. Not under any circumstances outside work. Even work would be difficult. But she couldn't allow herself to be so vulnerable to a man ever again.

"To new beginnings."

New beginnings? She wondered, clinking her glass with his. Ha, Bean's Creek had been her new beginning. Now she played by the stringent rules that kept her on the straight and narrow life path she'd chosen for herself.

Only with Grant had she ever questioned her direction.

She'd thought she could play and not pay a price. What she hadn't counted on was that in their game she wasn't the only player.

"And to playing by the rules," she added. Maybe it was perverse to say so. Certainly the look on Grant's face said her toast wasn't one that made him happy.

But she needed protecting from herself because he was so irresistible. Because she couldn't see him if she couldn't abide by her rules. More and more she was beginning to wonder. That scared her, made her think maybe she couldn't continue to see Grant.

Hating the cold hard truth, she pretended to be entranced by their surroundings. The moment the balloonist distracted Grant by pointing something out, she tossed the contents of her champagne glass over the side of the basket without having taken an actual sip. The balloonist stared at her as if she was a lunatic, but he didn't say anything, and when Grant turned to see what the man was looking at, Joni just shrugged.

She could have just told Grant she didn't drink, except then he'd have asked why and that wasn't something she intended to get into with him. Ever.

The balloon landed near a predestined spot and another Skyline worker met them and helped them out while the balloonist made adjustments inside the basket.

"Wow, this place is magnificent," she breathed, looking around them. Lush, tree-covered mountains in the distance, deep blue sky above them, soft green meadow beneath their feet.

If not for the fear that this was going to be her last day with Grant, she might think the setting just about perfect. Instead, the beauty of the place just seemed to mock her.

Still, she had today. One last day with Grant.

She'd been quiet way too long, Grant thought, holding Joni's hand as they walked several yards away from the balloon and watched the employees tie the basket down.

"Come on," he ordered, tugging her towards where he'd arranged for a romantic picnic. According to the person he'd talked to, they would have an hour of total privacy to eat and enjoy each other's company in the beauty of the North Carolina countryside. An hour where he and Joni could talk without any distractions.

"Where are we going?"

"Just over that rise there's a stream. Our dinner is there." He waggled his brows. "I worked up a hunger on the drive over."

She looked toward the rise, then gave him a mischievous grin. "I must have missed that. I don't remember you doing much work."

If she thought keeping his concentration on the road, keeping his hands on the steering-wheel rather than on her, had been easy, she needed to think again.

"You're right," he admitted, wrapping his arm around her waist. "I owe you one."

Acting nonchalant, she batted her lashes. "You owe me more than one."

Yes, he did. Lots more.

"Dozens," he promised, kissing the tip of her nose. Which was a mistake because putting his lips anywhere on her body just made him want to taste her all over.

"Dozens?" She looked impressed. "That's better."

"I can think of better."

Her gaze met his and all teasing ceased. "Me, too."

Grant fought the urge to toss her over his shoulder, carry her over the rise, and do better. Lots better.

He'd like to do better.

Their bodies were perfect. But them? He and her? They needed a chance she refused to give them.

He tugged on her hand, determined to see this through.

"Wow!" she exclaimed, coming to a complete stop when they came on the prepared picnic. "That was some prize package you won. This is amazing."

He wouldn't tell her he'd upgraded his package, put in custom requests, paid a small fortune for the additions. There wasn't any reason to. Seeing the excited look in her eyes made everything worthwhile.

She made everything worthwhile.

"Just as requested, your picnic dinner awaits," the Skyline employee named Kyle informed them, having finished at the balloon and having joined them.

A picturesque picnic complete with red and

white checked blanket had been spread out on a grassy area a hundred yards or so from where they were. A large basket overflowing with goodies sat on one corner. A smaller basket rested on the other corner.

"You have an hour before we have to be back up in the air," the man continued. "There's a cabin down that way." He pointed in the direction he meant. "To give our customers privacy, we'll be at the cabin until about five minutes prior to take-off. If you need a bathroom break or anything, you can head in that direction. We want you to enjoy your Skyline experience."

"Thank you," both Joni and Grant replied at the same time.

"You folks enjoy, and if you need anything, just give a holler."

"Will do," Grant agreed, watching as the man disappeared over the rise.

Joni squeezed his hand, her gaze eating him up as it raked down his body. "I'm starved. You?"

Oh, he was hungry all right. But not just for food. Or for her body for once, although the way she was looking at him was rapidly getting him there.

What he was starved for was answers to the dozens of questions running through his head, not the least of which was her reaction to him telling her he was falling in love with her.

There was probably a rule she'd forgotten to tell him about him wanting answers, but today wasn't about rules.

Today he was going to prise apart whatever held her back from a relationship with him.

CHAPTER ELEVEN

GRANT insisted on catering to Joni, made her sit while he examined the contents of the basket.

She started to argue, to insist on helping, but she'd realized he wanted to do this. That she wanted to let him. If today was her last day with him then she would have the full fantasy. Let a gorgeous man wait on her. Truth was, part of her still couldn't believe he wanted to, that he'd said what he had about wanting a real relationship with her.

"Looks good," he said when he had the food out of the basket and arranged on the blanket between them.

"Smells good, too." Joni inhaled deeply, eyeing the food with real appreciation. "I didn't realize how hungry I was."

"Flying works up an appetite."

Flying wasn't what had worked up her appetite. "Or something like that."

Meeting her gaze, Grant grinned. "Right. Let's eat."

The basket had been stuffed with the meal that Grant had pre-ordered. Fruit, cheese, grilled chicken, steamed vegetables, a chocolate dessert to die for—at least that was what Grant said the menu had stated.

Later, she agreed with the menu's claim. "Okay, this is phenomenal." She licked her spoon to make sure she didn't miss a trace of the chocolate delicacy. "We're in the middle of nowhere, and this is better than most restaurants. How did they do this?"

"I imagine they helicoptered the food in. Wouldn't take but a few minutes to get it here by 'copter. Although they could have driven it in." He proffered his laden with dessert spoon to her, smiling when she closed her mouth around the treat and moaned. "Regardless, we took the scenic route."

"That is so good," she said, shaking her head when he offered his last bite to her. "You eat it, please. The balloon may not be able to lift me to get us home as it is."

"You didn't eat that much. Here." He stuck the spoon in her mouth again, causing another meltdown of chocolate deliciousness.

"I ate more than my share. Thank you. Everything was wonderful." She lay back on the over-sized blanket, stared at the blue, blue sky, wondering how nature had so perfectly replicated the hue of Grant's eye color. If she would ever look at the sky on a perfect cloudless day and not think of him.

No, she wouldn't think of that. Not now.

"I'm so stuffed I may never move again." Glancing at him, she pointed her finger in a mock scold. "Don't even say it."

"What?"

"Whatever you were thinking." Her smile killed the effect of her words.

"I'm innocent, I tell you." Despite his claim, he didn't look any more innocent than he sounded—which wasn't at all.

"Right."

He lay back next to her, clasped her hand in his.

"Whatever shall we do for the next thirty minutes?" Despite her full belly, Joni started to roll over and kiss him, to spend the remaining time with her body entangled with his. After all, the workers had ensured their privacy and they'd never made love in the wide open countryside. Neither would they ever have opportunity after today because she really couldn't risk continuing their affair.

Her heart squeezed, skipping a beat. Desperate to feel his body against hers, she leaned towards him.

But rather than accept her kiss, he shook his head. "Talk to me, Joni."

Huh?

She was offering herself to him in the middle of paradise, and he wanted to talk? Really?

Okay, so they had already made love twice, but… Unsure what to think, she attempted to disentangle her fingers from his. He held on tight enough that she couldn't free her hand, yet not once did his grip hurt.

"Don't do that."

"Do what?" she asked, because she really didn't understand.

"Pull away from me. I don't mean from my hand. I mean you shutting me out."

"I don't shut you out."

"Sure you do," he countered, squeezing her hand. "Every time I try to move our relationship beyond the physical, you shut me out."

"You shouldn't attempt to move our relationship beyond physical. Let's be real, you and I are only physical. Once the chemistry fizzes, poof, we're gone like a puff of smoke."

"Do you really believe that?" He looked stunned and she found herself questioning so much. But even if he wanted more, how could she ever risk her career again? She couldn't. When they ended, who was to say he wouldn't turn on her the way Mark had? She liked her life in Bean's Creek, didn't want to start over somewhere else.

"Why wouldn't I?"

He lifted their twined hands and placed them on his chest just above his heart. "Because of this."

She shook her head. "I don't want to have this conversation."

"I'm sure you don't, but this conversation is overdue."

She didn't want to ever have this conversation. "Aren't you listening? You and I are just sex."

"If you believe that, you're lying to yourself. You and I have never just been about sex."

She started to deny his claim, but she couldn't. He was right. No matter how she wanted to label what was between them, no matter how she wanted to cling to a bunch of rules that had only served as a ruse for her to hide behind, she and Grant were about more than just sex.

"What is it you want from me?"

He gave her hand another gentle squeeze. "For you to talk to me."

"About?"

"About why you refuse to acknowledge that you and I are in a relationship together. About why we are so perfect together, yet you insist we are only physically attracted to each other. About whatever it is you're hiding from me. About whatever happened to you to make you not believe in love."

Emotions flooded through her. She didn't want to talk about the past. "Don't."

"Don't what?" he asked, his voice so gentle moisture stung her eyes.

"Don't ruin today," she pleaded.

Confusion shone in his blue eyes. "Talking to me about our relationship will ruin our day?"

"Yes."

"Why?"

"Because it's against the rules."

"Screw your rules, Joni. They were only words all along."

She swallowed hard. "You were just humoring me?"

"I was waiting for you to realize you were wrong."

"I'm not wrong." Her throat pinched tight, making breathing difficult.

"Which would mean that I am wrong to believe there is more between us than just sex?"

Joni closed her eyes, bit into her lower lip, then winced. Was he wrong? The wild thumping in her chest implied he was, but if that were the case then she'd only been fooling herself from the very beginning. Had she set herself up for heartache? Had she possibly jeopardized her career by becoming involved with another doctor? Someone the hospital would value much more than her if push came to shove?

What had she been thinking?

She hadn't been thinking. She'd been feeling.

Lust. That was all this was. Physical attraction. Yes, Grant was a good man. He was a responsible doctor who provided good care to his patients. He treated all the hospital staff with respect and courtesy. So of course she liked him.

Liking him didn't mean she loved him.

She wasn't in love with him.

She just wasn't. Love had hurt so much.

She glared at him, hardened her voice. "Not every woman is waiting for Prince Charming to come swooping into her life and carry her off on a white horse."

Not that such a creature even existed. Prince Charmings were as fictional as the fairies she collected.

"I don't believe they are. Just as not every man wants to settle down and marry someday. But most people do want someone to share their life with. Someone to talk to and discuss the day's events with. Someone to listen and hold your hand." He stroked his thumb across hers as if to stress his point. "Someone who cares what happens."

"You want that?" she gulped out, barely able to breathe.

"Yes, Joni, I want that." He inhaled sharply. "With you."

Why was her throat closing off? Why was her head spinning? Why was her heart racing a mile a minute? Why couldn't she just tell him to forget her rules and have that with her?

A fuzzy image of Mark's face danced through her mind. He'd told her he loved her, that he wanted to spend his life with her, that they'd marry and have babies together, that they'd grow old together. Instead, he'd cheated on her, wanted her to turn her back on her mother, and tried to destroy her career.

"If what we have isn't enough, we end right now."

Grant stared at Joni in disbelief. Seriously,

she'd let them end before she'd admit that what they had was much more than just sex?

Was he so wrong?

He wanted to take her in his arms and kiss her until she admitted she needed him.

But, then, that was the problem, wasn't it?

Joni did admit to needing him physically. Elsewhere in her life was where she wouldn't budge. She wanted their relationship in a neat little box that she could label as only sex.

He signed in frustration. "You haven't enjoyed today?"

"You know I did. But today is about sex."

Yeah, he hadn't meant for that to happen. Unfortunately he had trouble remembering that when she'd started touching him. Or met him at the door naked.

"We didn't have sex in the balloon." So he was reaching with that one, but they hadn't and not because he hadn't thought about it. A lot.

Apparently wanting to lighten their conversation, she gave him an impish grin. "Yet."

Her one little word sent his libido into hyperdrive, sent visions through his mind of him behind her, inside her, as they floated through the sky.

"Joni," he began, not wanting their conversation to turn sexual.

She rolled onto her side, ran her finger over his chest in a slow tease. "Face it, Grant. You and I are all about this right here." Her finger made an erotic sweep down his mid-section. "This powerful, magic pull between us that makes me want you inside me right now."

"Right now?" He gulped, wondering if she was trying to kill him.

"Oh, yeah." Her fingers were walking again. Lower and lower. She pushed against his chest, laying him flat on his back. Crawling on top of him, she smiled down at him. "I want you inside me."

A stronger man might resist her. Grant couldn't. Not when she rubbed herself against him and kissed him as if she needed him more than her next breath. Hell, he was only human.

And she was really hot.

"Dr. Bradley?" a voice called from way off in the distance. The balloonist. So much for guaranteed privacy. Probably wise the man was giving them warning way before they could see him. Very wise.

Joni quit moving, slid off him and back onto the blanket next to him. "You were saved by the bell."

"You think I wanted to be saved by the bell?"

She shook her head. "No, I think you wanted the same thing I wanted."

"What gave you that idea?"

She glanced at his jeans.

"You make a good point."

"Grant?"

He didn't like the seriousness in the way she said his name.

"On my rules…"

Neither did he like the word "rules" or that she felt she needed them with him.

"You do still agree to them, right?"

Had he ever really agreed to them?

"Because if you don't, I can't see you any more," she continued. "Not outside the hospital, I mean."

He hated this. Hated that she wouldn't let him

inside those walls she'd hidden behind. Maybe with time he'd scale them. Or knock them down completely. But he was tired of Joni's damned rules.

"Dr. Bradley?" the balloonist called again, this time from much closer. After promising complete privacy, Grant was a little irked that they were being interrupted.

"Over here. Where the picnic was set up," he called back, although surely the man knew exactly where he and Joni would be.

When the balloonist rushed over the rise, rosy cheeked and out of breath, Grant instantly knew something was wrong, that their privacy wasn't just idly being disturbed. He jumped to his feet and headed toward the man.

"Kyle was messing around outside the cabin and reached for something and was bit by a rattler," the man exclaimed breathlessly before Grant could ask.

"A snake?" Joni asked, also now on her feet.

The balloonist nodded. "He's at the cabin. I hated to leave him, but I didn't know what to do other than to come get you, Dr. Bradley."

"For the record," Grant said as they hurried toward the cabin, "I'm a pulmonologist."

"You still know what to do, though, right?" The man sounded worried, like he would somehow have to know if Grant didn't.

"I know." He'd never worked an actual snakebite case, but he did know the basics.

"Me, too," Joni piped up from where she ran beside them. "I worked the emergency room before I moved to Bean's Creek. We saw several snakebites during my time there."

Something else Grant hadn't known about her. That she'd worked in the emergency department at a hospital other than Bean's Creek. Where? he wondered. And why had she left? Did that have something to do with her need to try to put their relationship in a tidy box with boundaries and rules?

When they came upon the cabin, the man was half sitting, half lying on a rugged-looking leather sofa. Pale, he held a dish towel over his left hand. There was more blood on the towel than Grant would have expected from a snakebite.

"I feel like such a fool," he said when they rushed into the room.

"How long ago did the bite happen?" Joni asked, immediately taking the man's hand with care and elevating it. "You need to keep your hand elevated to the level of your heart."

Careful not to touch any of the bloody areas, Grant lifted the towel away from the man's hand.

"Maybe fifteen minutes ago." The man glanced toward his left hand and winced. "I didn't know I was supposed to have my hand elevated."

"Having the bite site elevated to the level of the heart helps to slow down envenomation." Grant began checking the bite site. There were two deep puncture wounds. Blood oozed from the man's hand. The snake had definitely been poisonous. Only poisonous snakes had fangs. Non-poisonous snake bites would show a row of teeth marks, not the fang punctures.

"Am I dying? I watch those television shows about people who shouldn't have survived and stuff." The man's voice cracked, sounding panicky. "I'm going to die, aren't I?"

"Those television shows show the dramatic

cases because that's what makes people tune in. Snakebites are serious business, but death from a snakebite, even a poisonous snakebite, is rare," Grant assured him, although the truth was the man's bite was serious. They were in the middle of nowhere with limited medical supplies and who knew how long it would take for the emergency helicopter to get to them to transport the patient to the hospital. He continued to assess the bite. Redness had begun spreading around the area. The man's entire hand was swollen.

Not seeing anything he could readily use to bind around the man's arm to also help slow down envenomation, Grant stripped off his T-shirt, took his keys out of his jeans, and jabbed a hole into the material. Using the hole as a starting point, he tore the material into a strip, then jerked it apart.

"I need to take your ring and watch off you. We don't want any jewelry cutting off circulation if you continue to swell," Joni told the man as she attempted to do so. With his hand and fingers already swollen, removing his wedding band wasn't easy. It took her squirting hand sanitizer on the area to add lubrication before the gold would budge.

While Joni's fingers remained on the bite victim's wrist, taking his pulse, Grant turned to the other Skyline employee. "Is there a first-aid kit? We need to see if there is a snakebite kit." Or anything else they could use to suction the wound.

The nervous man, who'd been standing just beyond the sofa, watching, pale faced, nodded and went to grab the first-aid kit.

Grant tied the material from his shirt around the man's forearm, not tight enough to cut off circulation but enough to slow down the spread of the venom.

"I feel really dizzy." Kyle shifted, sounding frightened. His movement caused a fresh wave of blood to ooze from the wound. The only good thing about the blood was that maybe some of the venom was being forced out along with the blood.

"Try to stay still, calm," Grant advised, because the man becoming excited, moving around a lot, would increase his circulation and speed up the spread of the venom.

Joni's gaze met his. "Heart rate is one hundred thirty. Respirations twenty."

Tachycardic and tachapneic. Not good. Most snakebites didn't cause the victim to go into shock, but it could happen, depending upon the amount of venom injected.

"Here's the first-aid kit." The balloonist almost tripped over his feet trying to get the kit to them.

"Go get him something to drink," Joni ordered the balloonist, taking the kit and opening it. She handed Grant a pair of latex gloves and donned a pair herself. "Preferably bottled water. We need to push fluid."

"I feel like I can't breathe."

Panic, shock, or a reaction to the venom?

"It's okay," Joni soothed after leaning in, listening closely to the man's chest then digging through the kit again. "Dr. Bradley's specialty is breathing. He's the best, and we're going to take good care of you." She turned to Grant and held up a small plastic package. "Look what I found."

A snakebite kit.

Handing him a disinfectant packet so he could clean the wound site, she tore open the sealed snakebite kit. She removed the extractor and handed the suction device to Grant while she began talking to their patient again, trying to calm him, carefully continuing to assess his breathing status.

Grant couldn't help but think how glad he was that Joni was there with him, for many reasons. She was a great nurse. A great woman. And they couldn't see each other any more if he didn't play by her rules?

He wanted to scream and rant and rave about how unfair she was being, that he was not a glorified booty call, that he wanted a real relationship, to make her see reason. Now wasn't the time, though. A man's life rested in their hands.

So he suctioned the wound, letting Joni's calm voice help calm him, too. The man was going into shock. They were in the middle of nowhere. The first-aid kit was basic. No epinephrine. Nothing to intubate the man if his airways closed. Not much of anything other than basic run-of-the-mill first-aid bandages and creams. He supposed he should be grateful someone had had the foresight to purchase a snakebite kit.

"Here's water. I got one for you and Doc, too."

Joni smiled at the balloonist, took the water, opened the lid, and encouraged the bite victim to start drinking. "You feel light-headed because your blood pressure is starting to drop. You need to take in fluid. As much fluid as you can stand. Drink up."

The man took the bottled water in his good hand and took a drink.

"Is there a defibrillator on the premises?" Joni asked the question as if it were no big deal, as if she was making casual conversation, but Grant knew better. She was wanting to be as prepared as possible for anything that came up with their patient.

The balloonist pointed toward a far wall. "That's what that is. We were trained, but I don't know that I could do it."

"Not a problem." She flashed a reassuring smile. "Dr. Bradley and I are more than qualified should need arise. Which isn't likely," she added for the victim's benefit.

The man had downed about half the bottled water. "My hand is twitching."

Yes, Grant had noticed the muscle spasms. A sign of neurotoxicity.

"That sometimes happens," Joni assured the man, patting his arm. "Do you have any other health problems? Are you on any medications?"

"I'm a walking pharmacy." Kyle took another swig of the water. "But I can't remember all the names. I have about ten different ones."

"Do you know what you take them for?"

"Diabetic problems, blood-pressure problems, my heart, and my blood."

"Your blood?" Grant wondered if Joni's stomach had clenched the way his just had.

"I have to take some of that rat-poison stuff because I've had blood clots in my legs in the past."

He was on anti-coagulation therapy to prevent the reoccurrence of clots. Not good.

"When was your last protime and INR test to see how thin your blood is?"

"A couple of months ago. I'm supposed to go every month. But it's always good. I missed last month." His gaze dropped to his swollen hand. "Didn't figure it would be a problem."

"You really need to have that checked every

month as so many things affect the level of medication in your system. It's easy for the blood to get too thin or too thick if your levels aren't monitored properly."

"Yeah, they told me that I can't eat greens any more because of that."

That explained why there'd been more bleeding than Grant would have expected. The man was on a blood-thinning agent. Great. One of the mechanisms of venom was to thin the blood.

The bite victim's risk of internal bleeding went way up.

So did Grant's heart rate.

They needed to get the man to the hospital Stat.

"How long did they say it would be before the 'copter got here?"

"Probably about twenty minutes."

"Twenty minutes?" Surely twenty minutes had already come and gone from the time the man would have made the call. Just fetching him and Joni and their trip back to the cabin probably had taken longer.

"Maybe there was another call or something," the balloonist offered.

"Maybe." Grant shook his head at the irony of it. He'd wanted time with Joni, time for them to get to know each other besides physically, and instead the romantic day he'd planned had turned into a crisis.

"How much of this do I have to drink?" The patient held up the water bottle. "Its making me feel like I want to throw up."

Between Joni's ultimatum and the guy's increasing symptoms and risk factors, Grant knew just how he felt.

Wondering how she and Grant's fabulous hot-air balloon trip had turned into wilderness medicine, Joni got up to search for something the man could use as a sick basin. She found a small white plastic trash bin and carried it next to the sofa.

She knelt next to Grant and reassessed Kyle's vitals. "Heart rate is one forty. Respirations still at twenty. Pulse is a little thready."

"Blood pressure is low." Grant spoke her thoughts out loud as he turned to the man. "Drink the rest of that water. Now."

The man nodded, his eyelids drooping.

"Drink," Joni ordered in a voice Grant would

probably say was her bossy voice. The man did so, finishing off what remained in his plastic bottle. She handed him one of the bottles the balloonist had brought for her and Grant. "Here's another. Drink."

The man grimaced. "I'll puke if I do."

"Puke into the garbage container, then, because you need to be drinking."

"I've suctioned out everything I can get."

Joni looked at him. Something she'd been trying not to do. Grant was always potent. She always wanted him. But Grant shirtless? Oh, my. Even in a crisis she wasn't immune enough not to notice that the man had a beautiful body. Her body wasn't strong enough not to be aware that he was so close.

Crazy. Not only were they in a crisis but they were also sort of in the middle of a fight. Why was she noticing how hot he was when he hadn't agreed to keep playing by her rules? When she didn't know where things stood with them?

"Then we just keep him stable until the rescue crew arrives," she said, looking directly into Grant's blue eyes and having a flashback to when they had been lying on the blanket, staring up at the sky, not having a care in the world except each other.

"Joni." His one word conveyed so much, conveyed all that she was thinking because she knew he was right back in that meadow with her. How did that work? That connection between them that allowed them to so readily read each other?

Her gaze went back to her patient and her heart almost stopped. Blood was trickling from the man's nose.

Not wanting to alarm him, her gaze went back to Grant's.

"Why is his nose bleeding?" the balloonist asked.

So much for not alarming their patient. The man wiped his nose, saw the blood, and became agitated. "I'm dying, aren't I? That's why you were asking about my medications."

"You're blood is just a little too thin, that's all," Joni assured him at the same time as Grant tried to get the man to lie back down.

"You've got to stay calm," Grant advised. "If

you're up moving around, any venom I couldn't get out will spread faster."

"If my nose is bleeding, I'd say it's already spread."

"Is he dying?" the balloonist asked, looking paler and paler.

Joni gave him a "get it together and be quiet" look, then pointed to a chair across the room. "Sit down, and be ready to help."

The last thing they needed was for him to pass out and give himself a concussion. One patient was more than enough.

When the balloonist had done as ordered, she turned back to her patient, whom Grant was talking to and assessing.

"There are different aspects of what the snake's venom does. One is to thin the blood, another is to suppress your central nervous system, which is why you're having that little muscle twitch in your hand. The third is to cause breakdown of tissue." Grant's voice was calm, steady. He talked to distract the man from his panic more than to actually educate him on snakebites.

"I feel really light-headed."

Joni wished she had a way to measure Kyle's blood pressure. She knew the readings would be low, that his body was in shock.

She packed his nostril with gauze from the first-aid kit in the hope of stopping the bleeding. Help would arrive soon so the man could be transported to the hospital and anti-venom could be administered.

As if her prayers were answered, a low buzz could be heard in the distance.

"Thank God," she breathed as the sound grew louder and louder.

"Amen," Grant seconded.

Once aboard the rescue helicopter, Joni had nothing to do except sit on her hands.

The paramedics had taken over Kyle's care, so really even Grant was unnecessary at this point. He sat next to her with nothing more to do than to observe as well.

"So much for our romantic sunset flight, eh?"

Joni glanced out the helicopter's window. The sun was beginning to settle behind the mountains. Brilliant oranges, reds, blues, pinks, and yellows streaked the sky.

"For whatever its worth, the sunset is gorgeous."

He grinned. The noise from the helicopter made further conversation difficult, so they sat in silence during the trip to the closest emergency department.

When they arrived at the hospital, everything blurred. Joni and Grant both offered to help any way they could, but the emergency room doctor had taken over and they were superfluous.

"Dr. Bradley, we admitted a patient to ICU earlier. While you're here you may want to peek in on them," Cindy, the emergency department nurse, told him, glancing curiously back and forth between Grant and Joni.

Joni didn't meet the woman's eyes, wanted to go and hide, but, really, what was the point? Word would be all over the hospital that she and Grant had been out on a balloon ride together. Great.

Grant asked the woman a few questions about the admitted patient, then turned to Joni. "You okay waiting for a few minutes?"

"Of course, Dr. Bradley."

She spoke so formally that Grant winced. Still, what had he expected? That she'd bat her lashes at him and say, "Sure, honey, anything you want"? Hardly. The entire emergency department probably thought something was going on between them now. Ugh. Why hadn't she thought of this earlier when they'd climbed aboard the rescue helicopter? Then again, it wasn't as if they could have flown the balloon back themselves and the balloonist was all shaken up. No way would she have wanted to float through the sky at his mercy.

"Joni?"

Shocked, Joni glanced up to see an older version of herself in the closest curtain-partitioned bay. "Mom? What are you doing here? Is everything okay?"

She glanced back and forth between the tired-appearing woman lying on the hospital bed and her stepfather, who held his wife's hand.

"I'm fine. I tripped and fell off the porch. Chris thought I might have broken something."

Tripped? Fell off the porch? Warning bells blared in Joni's head. "You weren't...?" She couldn't finish her question. Not with her so aware that Grant had followed her into her mother's bay, that he listened to every word being said. She didn't want him to know, didn't want to risk a repeat of history.

Her mother's face paled.

"No, she wasn't drinking," Joni's stepfather assured her, lifting his wife's hand to his lips and pressing a kiss to skin. "You'd be proud and can tell everyone at your next AA meeting that she even told the E.R. doctor that if her ankle was broken, she didn't want any narcotic pain medications because she was a recovering alcoholic and an addict."

There it was. Those awful words. That awful truth from her past. Out in the open for Grant to hear and know. Out in the open for her fellow hospital co-workers to hear and know.

Joni Thompson's mother was an alcoholic and an addict.

Her whole life she'd dealt with that fact, loved her mother, and had forgiven her years ago for the pain and anguish she'd suffered as a child and teen with a parent who'd stayed intoxicated more often than not.

For the briefest moment she resented the public announcement of her mother's past sins. But only for the briefest of moments. Then she met Grant's startled blue eyes head on, took in the disgust that settled onto his face. She'd known, hadn't she? That he would have no compassion or sympathy for her mother? Fine. Who needed him, anyway? She lifted her chin high, daring him to say a single derogatory word, because if he so much as uttered a single one she was liable to hit him.

He didn't. He just stared at Joni, her mother, then shook his head as if he couldn't take another moment, and walked away without a word.

Joni knew she talked to her mother and stepfather for several more minutes, that she didn't leave until the X-ray films showed that her mother had just severely sprained her ankle, not sustained any fractures, until she knew her stepfather didn't need her help getting her mother home and settled.

She also knew she and Grant wouldn't be picking up where they'd left their conversation at their picnic.

There was no need.

He wouldn't be playing by any rules.

He wouldn't be playing at all.

Thank goodness she'd had her rules to protect her or she'd swear that ache in her chest was her heart breaking.

CHAPTER TWELVE

USING all her might, Joni pressed against her patient's chest in repetitive motions, giving two breaths via the CPR bag to every thirty compressions.

Samantha had gone after the crash cart and to call the code. Her friend couldn't have been gone more than a few seconds, but already time seemed to have stopped.

Yet every second that passed that she couldn't get Mr. Gold's heart to jump-start increased the odds that he wouldn't come back.

Her arms wobbled, feeling like water had replaced her muscles. She'd done CPR before, never failed to be amazed at how much energy was required to perform the chest compressions correctly. No matter, Samantha would be back in the room soon, would inject Mr. Gold with medication and together they'd defibrillate the man in the hope they weren't too late.

Seconds later whoever was on call as code physician would arrive, would take charge of the code, and Joni could react to orders rather than have a man's life in her hands, literally.

Please let his heart beat. Please let him take a breath.

She leaned down, listened and felt for a breath. Nothing. She checked for a heartbeat. No pulse.

She started another set of compressions, wondering why her workout routine hadn't prepared her in the slightest for this because surely if it had, her arms wouldn't be aching so.

"Here, let me."

Relief and a million other emotions washed over her as Grant moved to the other side of the patient and took over compressions while she continued respirations.

"Tell me what happened." His chest compressions were perfect, perfect depth, perfect rhythm, seemingly effortless from his strong arms.

"I was doing neuro checks when his eyes rolled

back. His telemetry went off. No heartbeat. No respirations. I called for help and started CPR." She squeezed the bag to give the man a puff of air in perfect sync with Grant's sets of compressions. "Samantha was in the next room, came to check, and she's gone to call the code and get the crash cart."

On cue, the code announcement came over the hospital intercom system. Samantha rushed back into the room. Altogether her friend hadn't been out of the room a full minute, but Joni was so relieved to see her friend that weeks could have passed.

Grant began issuing orders while Samantha injected epinephrine into Mr. Gold and hooked him to the defibrillator.

"All clear. Now."

Samantha set off the charge. Mr. Gold's body jumped, but no heartbeat. Nothing.

"All clear. Again."

Over and over they tried to revive their patient, but nothing. After long, exhausting minutes Grant called the code to an end.

Joni dealt with death routinely. Working in ICU, how could she not? But never did she lose a patient that her own heart didn't ache over the loss. Each patient was someone's mother or father, someone's brother or sister, someone's son or daughter, was the person someone's heart was most connected to. Each death marked a life that had affected many people's lives.

She'd fought tears the last few minutes of their efforts to save Mr. Gold. Only she wasn't sure if the moisture stinging her eyes was just for the man's life that had slipped away or for the loss of Grant from her life.

They might not have had a real relationship, but somehow every aspect of her life had gotten all tangled up with him and she missed him. Missed him so fiercely that each night for the past two weeks she'd cried herself to sleep and woken up with her pillow damp from even more tears.

She imagined she looked a wreck. Definitely, Samantha, Brooke, and several others commented on how worried they were about her. But what could she say? That she'd lost someone she'd never really had? That Grant had learned of her mother's problems and hightailed it out of her life?

As soon as she could sneak away from Mr. Gold's room, she did. Finding an empty patient room, she let the tears fall, not trying to stop them.

She cried for Mr. Gold, for his family, for his friends. She cried for herself and the hospital staff that hadn't been able to save him. She wanted to save every patient.

Impossible, she knew. Death was inevitable for every person. But with each patient she lost she felt disappointment, a sense of failure, had a moment of what if she'd gotten to the person earlier, realized what was happening sooner, somehow have done something that might have brought on a different, better result.

Life was full of what-ifs.

What if she'd met Grant first, hadn't had the scars of her relationship with Mark? What if she'd trusted in him and been willing to risk a real relationship with him? What if she went to him and begged him to let her back into his life because she only felt half-alive without him by her side?

"You okay?"

"I'm fine." Joni immediately sat up straighter, swiped at her tears. Why had Grant followed her? For two weeks he'd not said a word to her, or sent a single text, or left any "secret admirer" gifts or notes. Nothing. So why was he here now when she felt so weak? When she wanted nothing more than to lay her head on his shoulder and breathe in the scent of him?

Grant stared at her, shook his head. "No, you're not. Come here."

She didn't move, couldn't seem to get her legs to co-operate with the mixed signals her brain and heart were sending. Don't budge, her brain urged. Lean on him, her heart pleaded.

When she didn't move, Grant took her hand, pulled her up from the chair and into his arms and held her.

Tight. As if she mattered. As if he hadn't walked out of that emergency room and her life.

Fresh tears began to flow.

She loved him. Loved this wonderful, beautiful man who was holding her so close, comforting her, even though he didn't want her any more.

Even though he'd walked away from her. How could she love someone so intolerant of other's flaws? What right did he have to judge her mother?

She pulled away. "No, really, I'm fine. Just leave me alone."

Lips tightening into a fine line, he stared at her. "Joni?"

Knowing she had to put some space between them, she shook her head. "I just needed a minute to compose myself. Sometimes I have to do that after losing a patient."

"Understandable," he said slowly, studying her so intently she wanted to squirm. "You're a great nurse, care about your patients."

She nodded. "I can't do this, Grant."

His jaw worked back and forth as he silently regarded her. She'd expected him to say something but he just stood staring at her, waiting for her to elaborate. Sometimes she'd swear the man had the patience of Job.

"This has been fun, but…" But what? She didn't want more? Ha, she wanted lots more. That was the problem. She wanted more from him but had been too scared to admit it even to herself until he'd walked away. "I can't pretend we're friends when we're not. I can't pretend nothing happened between us when it did. Please just go away and leave me alone."

Grant stepped back, looking at her as if she carried the plague.

"Fine." He shrugged, sounding as if he didn't really care one way or the other. "If that's what you want, that's what I'll give you. This whole relationship has been about what you want anyway."

His words stung. Stung painfully sharp. Her pride kicked in.

"I didn't hear you complaining about not getting what you wanted when we were in bed. Not once did I hear a single complaint."

"Take note, Joni." His eyes bored into her, glittering with anger. "I'm complaining now. I'm complaining that you are the most selfishly independent woman I've ever met. I'm complaining that when I was willing to give us a real chance, you put stupid rules in place that prevented us from ever having a chance at anything more. I'm complaining that you never let me in, never told me about your problems."

His voice grew angrier and angrier with each new complaint, searing into Joni's chest with icy coldness. "I'm complaining that you would hide something as major as addiction from me. How could you do that, knowing how I felt? How could you have deceived me about something so horrible?"

His words shredded the tattered remains of Joni's heart.

She wanted to scream at him, wanted to demand how he could have professed to be falling in love with her and later that same day to have turned your back on her because of her mother's problems? What did he expect? For her to turn her back on her mother? Why would she do that after her mother had been sober for almost five years? Not that she would even if her mother fell back into the same habits. You didn't turn your back on people you loved no matter what their problems were. Not ever.

Grant didn't love her. He'd just been caught up in the fantasy of their attraction to each other. Ha, for once she could honestly say just the sight of him disgusted her.

"Complaints duly noted." Body stiff, she stared back at him, watching as more and more angry color stained his face. "Aren't you lucky you don't have to ever deal with my silly rules ever again? Goodbye, Grant."

With that, she marched out of the room, head held high, proud that this time she'd been the one to walk away.

Later she'd deal with the doubts burning in her chest. Much later.

Or maybe never, because she didn't want to examine too closely the thought of Grant not being a part of her life, that maybe she was wrong, that she should have opened up to him, talked to him, told him her fears and vulnerabilities.

At least she still had her career this time. Because as angry as Grant was at her, she didn't believe he'd turn on her, lie to her boss and try to get her fired.

Then again, she'd been wrong before.

"So how's your love life?"

Joni grimaced at Mrs. Sain's question. She so

didn't want to have this conversation, but had known when she'd seen Mrs. Sain's name on the schedule that she wouldn't be able to avoid questions about Grant. "Not that it's any of your business, but I don't have a love life."

What was she saying? She'd never had a love life. A sex life, yes. Love life, no.

"What happened with you and Doc?"

Really, the woman was too much. Didn't she know asking such questions just wasn't polite? Or did such things not matter so much once you reached a certain age in life?

Maybe not, because Mrs. Sain didn't look in the slightest apologetic or embarrassed, just curious.

"Well? Don't even tell me that you blew it with my hunky doctor. Surely you're smarter than that."

"Surely," Joni agreed, finishing the woman's morning vitals.

"You blew it, didn't you? So what did you do?"

"Nothing much. Just told him to leave me alone."

"What?" The woman looked appalled. "He listened?"

"Yes. He listened. Why wouldn't he?"

The older woman shook her head, obviously disgusted with both of them. Good, maybe the older lady would quit asking questions and reminding her of what she fought really hard not to think of—Grant. Not that she succeeded much. Odd how not trying to think of something meant constantly thinking of that something.

Mrs. Sain gave a disgusted grunt, mumbled something under her breath.

Joni sighed, knowing she was going to regret her next words. "Go ahead. Say whatever it is you're thinking. I know you want to so don't start holding back now."

"You're an idiot."

Joni didn't know whether to laugh or cry at the woman's observation. "Probably."

"No probably to it. You are," Mrs. Sain declared, matter-of-factly. "That man is crazy about you and has been trying to win your heart for weeks."

"That's just sexual attraction." Why was she admitting this out loud? Really, she had lost her mind.

"Lucky you."

Yeah, lucky her. She plopped down into the chair next to Mrs. Sain's bed. Only she wasn't having sex with Grant any more. Instead, she was spending a lot of time recalling all the wonderful times she'd had with Grant. Times she'd classified as just sex but they hadn't been. Just sex would have been Grant leaving the moment they'd finished. Instead he'd held her for hours, talking, stroking her hair, her skin, kissing her so gently that he might have thought her fragile.

Her rules had been a joke, hadn't protected a thing, especially not her heart.

Wait! She wasn't supposed to be thinking about Grant.

Don't think about Grant. Don't think about Grant. Don't think about Grant... Oh! What was the use? She thought about him all the time whether she wanted to or not.

She missed him, deep down as if she'd lost a vital part of herself missed him.

"Now that you've told him to leave you alone, and he is, how are you going to win him back?"

Win him back? "I didn't say I wanted him back."

"I may be old, but I'm not blind."

"Or mute."

The older woman cackled with laughter, which triggered a coughing spell. Joni beat on her back, trying to help clear the mucus. Finally, Mrs. Sain was breathing semi-regularly again.

"Let's not do that again," Joni advised, assessing the woman's breathing pattern and oxygen saturation.

"Agreed."

"I'll have the respiratory therapist come do your breathing treatment, see if we can't get your airways cleared."

"Maybe you should just put a call in to my lung doctor. Pretty sure he could clear my airways better than any therapist. Maybe he could clear a few things for you, too."

Joni smiled at the older woman's gumption. "You do realize you're my patient, not my shrink, right?"

"Do you need a shrink?"

Did she? Goodness knew, her mind had been everywhere since she'd walked away from Grant.

She'd only caught rare glimpses of him at the

hospital. Which meant he was avoiding her, just as she was avoiding him.

Which was for the best. Having to see him all the time and knowing she'd never touch him again would be so much worse. At least she figured it would be. At the moment she did long to see him. To put her eyeballs on him and soak in his features.

She missed him.

Missed everything about him.

Especially his smile. The smile he reserved just for her.

"It really is his smile, you know," she said with a wistful sigh.

"I know," Mrs. Sain agreed. "The man's smile is positively lethal. You going to woo him back?"

"Woo him?" Joni grimaced, plopping back down in the chair she'd occupied prior to Mrs. Sain's coughing spell. "I wouldn't know where to begin."

Mrs. Sain's white eyebrows lifted. "You've never wooed a man?"

Before she'd learned that he'd been sleeping around for most of their relationship, she'd wanted to hang on to Mark, but she hadn't ever wooed him, had she? Perhaps she'd tried, but, if so, she'd failed.

She'd loved him, but now she knew better. He'd used her. As if shattering her heart hadn't been enough, he'd undermined her job, reporting her for supposed patient negligence, for supposed use of narcotics while on duty, leaving her utterly devastated personally and professionally.

Professionally, she'd recovered as the claims hadn't been true. Still, by the time the investigation had ended, she'd lost all joy in her job, all respect for the hospital board that had stood behind the acclaimed doctor who'd made the claims rather than a mere nurse. She'd needed a change, had moved to Bean's Creek, taken her mother with her, and started over.

Personally, she'd thought she had recovered, too. She'd thought she'd put all the pieces back together. But what she'd done was piece together a brick wall to hide behind. For the past five years she'd been hiding, afraid to live. No one had even tempted her to step out from behind her protective shield until she'd met the devil him-self—Grant. Only he hadn't been a devil at all. Far from it.

He'd been her saving grace and she'd been too blind to see the truth. She'd attempted to shield herself with rules. Rules meant to provide a barrier to protect her heart.

Rules that hadn't barricaded a thing.

"Tell him the truth," a crotchety old voice broke into her thoughts and advised.

"The truth?" She stared at Mrs. Sain in confusion.

"That you love him and want him back."

"He wants nothing to do with me." He didn't. He'd made no effort to see her, had accepted her request to leave her alone quite easily. She might have been the one to say goodbye, but he'd been the first to walk away that night at the E.R. Even if she'd doubted herself a thousand times since, he'd let her go, let her say goodbye. Then again, had she given him a choice? Had she even listened to anything he'd said or had she only been trying to scramble back behind her protective walls? "I pushed him away."

Mrs. Sain adjusted her nasal cannula, taking a deep breath. "Tell him you made a mistake. Ask him for his forgiveness."

"Why would he forgive me?"

Even with her wrinkled face it wasn't difficult to decipher Mrs. Sain's "duh" expression. "Because he loves you and wants you back?"

If only.

"I wish he did," Joni admitted on a wistful sigh. She rose to her feet because she'd dallied long enough and needed to get back to check on her other patient. Wishes were a waste of time.

"Do you?"

Joni's heart stopped. She turned slowly toward the door. Grant stood there, looking wonderful in his blue hospital scrubs that so perfectly matched his eyes. His beautiful eyes that she had missed looking into so much.

How long had he been standing there? Had Mrs. Sain seen him and not said anything? Probably, the wily old woman thought she knew best.

Joni opened her mouth to speak, but nothing

came out. Not a single sound. If she admitted that she really did wish he loved her and wanted her back, he'd probably laugh at her, remind her that she'd been the one to insist that they have a sex-only relationship. He'd probably tell her that he couldn't deal with her attending AA with her mother regularly and being her mother's number-one support system—although, honestly, she wasn't so sure about that one any more as her stepfather seemed to have a happy handle on things. He'd probably tell her that it served her right that she wanted him to love her because he'd tried to have a relationship with her and she'd been too scared to risk it. She'd stopped him at every turn, insisting they abide by her rules. Because she'd been afraid to risk love.

Now she'd lost him.

"What purpose would it serve if I loved you and wanted a woman back who only wants me for sex?"

"I never said that."

His brow lifted. "Didn't you?"

"Not in so many words, but yes," she admitted, face on fire. "I guess I did essentially say that."

Joni glanced toward Mrs. Sain, who was practically rubbing her hands together in glee. They shouldn't be having this conversation in front of her. Maybe they shouldn't be having this conversation at all.

Yet her heart wouldn't let her walk away. Not this time.

Sure, she'd be made a fool, just as she had been with Mark. Sure, Grant would probably laugh at her. But at least she'd know that she put her heart out there, that she had breathed life back into her body and lived.

And loved.

And risked everything for that love.

This time she knew that despite the fact that she truly loved Grant, she wouldn't bury herself away the way she had after the demise of her relationship with Mark.

Loving Grant had made her stronger, more capable of facing the rest of her life with arms open wide.

Yes, she'd lost her mind right along with her heart, but she loved this man and she wouldn't cower. Not ever again.

"Yes." She held her head high. "I wish you loved me and wanted me back."

Grant almost slid to the hospital floor in a surprised heap. He couldn't believe his ears. Was Joni really saying words he'd dreamed of her saying for weeks?

Then again, maybe she just missed the sex.

Definitely, he could understand that. Their bodies did phenomenal things together. Just being near her had every cell in his body standing at attention.

But they had bigger problems than just whether or not she'd realized there was more between them than sex. She was an addict. For weeks now he'd lain awake trying to come up with a solution to Joni's problem, to come up with a way for her not to end up as Ashley had. Apparently, she and her mother were in Alcoholics Anonymous together, perhaps even other rehab programs as well. How long had she been clean? How long had her mother? Back and forth he'd battled whether or not he could risk another Ashley. At times he knew he was strong enough to stand by Joni, to encourage her to make the right choices. At others he wondered if he could watch another woman he loved destroy herself.

"This is better than any soap opera I ever watched."

Grant glanced away from Joni at Mrs. Sain's observation. The woman's face glowed with excitement, but this was a conversation better done in private. He and Joni couldn't discuss the real issues with another person privy to the private details.

"Come with me," he ordered Joni, then told his patient, "I'll be back to check on you later."

"No rush, Doc. Take your time. Ain't as if I have anywhere to go."

Without waiting to see if Joni followed, Grant turned, left the room, and waited in the hallway.

"Grant, I…" She stopped next to him, stared at her feet, took a deep breath, and met his eyes. "I want you in my life."

"As your lover?"

"Yes," she immediately answered, her gaze searching his.

"If that's the only way you'll have me, then,

yes, be my lover, Grant," she whispered, taking his hand and lacing their fingers. "But you should know that I'll spend every moment of the rest of my life trying to make you love me."

Grant's heart quickened, pumped hard against his ribcage. "There's no need."

Her hand fell from his, her face tightening. "Then I've lost you for ever?"

"You misunderstand." He lifted her chin, forced her to meet his gaze. "There's no need for you to try to make me love you, because I already do."

Gaze lifting to his, her eyes glittered with moisture. "You do?"

He brushed his fingertip across her cheek, catching a single teardrop that had trickled down her face. "I tried telling you on the day of our Skyline trip, but you didn't want to hear what I was saying."

"I thought… Never mind what I thought. I wasn't ready to hear."

"I noticed. But that didn't make my words any less true." He cupped her face, stared straight into her eyes. "I love you, Joni Thompson. Now and for ever. I love you, but I'm not sure love is enough."

Joni's heart swelled, threatening to burst out of her chest, then careened at his final words.

"I lived with a woman before moving here. I loved her, planned to marry her, but about a year into our relationship I started noticing things, how much she drank, how many pills she popped. Unfortunately, I didn't see the half of it. I should have gotten out then, but I thought I could cure her."

He'd lived with an addict? That was why he'd felt the way he had about Kathy Conner? Why he'd walked away when he'd learned about her mother? Not because he hadn't loved her but because he hadn't been able to deal with having another addict in his life.

"I couldn't cure her, just as I wouldn't be able to cure you, Joni, and I don't know that I could bear watching you destroy yourself, but I can't not try, because I need you in my life."

"I won't turn my back on my mother," she interrupted, knowing she was sealing her fate but also knowing she had to lay all the facts on the line. "She doesn't need as much from me these days as she's been sober for almost five years, and especially not since she met and married my stepfather. But if she relapsed, if she needed me, I'd be at her side without question. Always." What he'd last said sank in. "Me?"

"Your mother?" he asked at the same time.

"I do not and neither have I ever used drugs of any kind. I was falsely accused once by someone I loved, but he was wrong."

"He was a fool," Grant said with such conviction Joni laughed.

"He was an esteemed doctor I had an affair with and it cost me my self-respect and my job."

"Like I said, he was a fool." He cupped her face. "I love you, Joni."

She'd heard the words before, heard them from Mark, but never had she heard them sincerely, never had she heard them from one heart to her own.

Grant loved her.

She could see the truth in his eyes, in the sweetness of the way he wiped away her tear.

"I love you, too." Joy filled her body and without thought she flung her arms around his neck, kissed him. "I've missed you! Oh, Grant, I've missed you so much."

"I've missed you, too." Grant seemed a bit stunned at her show of public affection, but kissed her back with a quick kiss to her mouth.

Embarrassed by her unprofessional act right in the middle of the ICU hallway, knowing she'd probably embarrassed him, too, Joni bowed her head.

"I'm sorry. I shouldn't have done that," she apologized, wondering at her crazy zig-zagging emotions.

"Look at me," he ordered her, lifting her face to his.

She did so.

"Don't ever be sorry for that. Not ever. Because I'm not." He closed his eyes, took a deep breath. "I'm yours, Joni. All of me. Any time you want me, I'm yours. Just yours."

She nodded, becoming more and more aware of their surroundings. They stood in the open hallway of the ICU. Anyone could see them. Everyone could see them.

"But I..."

"But you are mine, too." As if to prove his point, he cupped her face again, stared into her eyes. "Mine to touch. Just mine. No supply closet required."

Unable to find the power to speak, she nodded again.

"And, Joni?"

She met his gaze.

"This time I'm making the rules."

Not believing the sheer happiness jolting through her, she bit back a smile. "Oh? What kind of rules?"

"Rules of engagement, because I want you to be mine for ever."

Joni's eyes widened. Her jaw dropped. Was he?

"I may be rushing things, but I don't want to wait. Neither do I want there to be any question about what it is I want from you. I want everything. My first rule is that we go tomorrow and buy you the biggest, gaudiest diamond we can find so no one can miss that you are taken."

"But I don't need—"

He shook his head at her, interrupting. "My second rule is that we don't have sex again until your last name is the same as mine."

"I don't think—"

"No worries, Joni, love. I'm just ensuring that we have a really short engagement."

"I still don't—"

"And my third rule," he continued, not letting her finish, "is that you introduce me to your mother. Tonight. After we get off work, we'll go, tell her our news."

Joni stared at him in amazement.

"And my fourth rule, the most important rule of all, is that we love each other for ever."

No longer caring that they stood in the hallway, Joni wrapped her arms around his neck. "Are those all your rules, Dr. Bradley, or do you get to make more up along the way?"

"Depends." His mouth hovered close to hers. "On?"

"Whether or not you agree to the first four rules of our engagement."

"And if I don't?"

"You have to. Not agreeing is against the rules and I know how you feel about rules."

"That they are meant to be broken?" she teased, loving the way he looked at her, the way his eyes danced.

"Not my rules." His lips met hers, kissing her until she was breathless, until clapping sounded all around her.

Joni pulled back, smiled at Samantha and her other co-workers.

"Well, answer the poor man," Samantha ordered. "And you are not allowed to say no."

Joni started to point out that her friend was a good one to talk but, unlike Samantha, Joni didn't want to say no. She wanted Grant. For ever.

She looked straight into his sky-blue eyes. "It's your smile, you know."

"My smile?"

She nodded. "Oh, yes. Your smile is why I accept your rules of engagement."

"And here I thought it was because you loved me."

"I do love you, Grant, but it's your smile, the

one you reserve just for me, that takes my breath away."

Grant smiled.

* * * * *

Mills & Boon® Large Print
Medical

July

THE SURGEON'S DOORSTEP BABY — Marion Lennox
DARE SHE DREAM OF FOREVER? — Lucy Clark
CRAVING HER SOLDIER'S TOUCH — Wendy S. Marcus
SECRETS OF A SHY SOCIALITE — Wendy S. Marcus
BREAKING THE PLAYBOY'S RULES — Emily Forbes
HOT-SHOT DOC COMES TO TOWN — Susan Carlisle

August

THE BROODING DOC'S REDEMPTION — Kate Hardy
AN INESCAPABLE TEMPTATION — Scarlet Wilson
REVEALING THE REAL DR ROBINSON — Dianne Drake
THE REBEL AND MISS JONES — Annie Claydon
THE SON THAT CHANGED HIS LIFE — Jennifer Taylor
SWALLOWBROOK'S WEDDING OF THE YEAR — Abigail Gordon

September

NYC ANGELS: REDEEMING THE PLAYBOY — Carol Marinelli
NYC ANGELS: HEIRESS'S BABY SCANDAL — Janice Lynn
ST PIRAN'S: THE WEDDING! — Alison Roberts
SYDNEY HARBOUR HOSPITAL: EVIE'S BOMBSHELL — Amy Andrews
THE PRINCE WHO CHARMED HER — Fiona McArthur
HIS HIDDEN AMERICAN BEAUTY — Connie Cox